P9-CQH-065

She had to get out of there before she said something she regretted.

Or before *he* did, because the intensity of his gaze was almost…unnerving. Just the sight of Javier lying in bed, watching her like that, as if he was going to slide over to make room for her to join him…

Oh, for the love of Pete. The man was recuperating from near-fatal injuries. He certainly wasn't having those kinds of thoughts.

So why in creation was she?

Dear Reader,

I hope you like this new Fortunes of Texas series as much as I do. It was fun to return to Red Rock and revisit old "friends" as well as meet some new ones.

In *A Real Live Cowboy* (April 2009), J. R. Fortune fell in love with Isabella Mendoza. I'd mentioned that she had a brother, Javier. So you can imagine how exciting it was to be able to tell Javier's story and help him find his own happy ever after.

Of course, the poor man nearly died when the tornado struck Red Rock two months ago. The near-death experience and the long road back to recovery have taken an emotional toll on him, and the only bright spot in his day is when Leah Roberts, a lovely auburn-haired Florence Nightingale, enters his room.

As Leah's handsome patient heals, he begins to revert back to the man he once was—the kind of man who could prove to be the worst thing to ever happen to her... or the best.

So sit back and enjoy the romance that's about to unfold.

Happy reading!

Judy

MENDOZA'S MIRACLE

JUDY DUARTE

Harlequin®

SPECIAL EDITION

If you purchased this book without a cover you should be aware that this book is stolen property. It was reported as "unsold and destroyed" to the publisher, and neither the author nor the publisher has received any payment for this "stripped book."

Special thanks and acknowledgment to Judy Duarte
for her contribution to
The Fortunes of Texas: Whirlwind Romance continuity.

ISBN-13: 978-0-373-65655-4

Recycling programs
for this product may
not exist in your area.

MENDOZA'S MIRACLE

Copyright © 2012 by Harlequin Books S.A.

All rights reserved. Except for use in any review, the reproduction or utilization of this work in whole or in part in any form by any electronic, mechanical or other means, now known or hereafter invented, including xerography, photocopying and recording, or in any information storage or retrieval system, is forbidden without the written permission of the publisher, Harlequin Enterprises Limited, 225 Duncan Mill Road, Don Mills, Ontario M3B 3K9, Canada.

This is a work of fiction. Names, characters, places and incidents are either the product of the author's imagination or are used fictitiously, and any resemblance to actual persons, living or dead, business establishments, events or locales is entirely coincidental.

This edition published by arrangement with Harlequin Books S.A.

For questions and comments about the quality of this book please contact us at Customer_eCare@Harlequin.ca.

® and TM are trademarks of Harlequin Books S.A., used under license. Trademarks indicated with ® are registered in the United States Patent and Trademark Office, the Canadian Trade Marks Office and in other countries.

www.Harlequin.com

Printed in U.S.A.

JUDY DUARTE

always knew there was a book inside her, but since English was her least-favorite subject in school, she never considered herself a writer. An avid reader who enjoys a happy ending, Judy couldn't shake the dream of creating a book of her own.

Her dream became a reality in March 2002, when Silhouette Special Edition released her first book, *Cowboy Courage.* Since then she has published more than twenty novels.

Her stories have touched the hearts of readers around the world. And in July 2005 Judy won a prestigious Readers' Choice Award for *The Rich Man's Son.*

Judy makes her home near the beach in Southern California. When she's not cooped up in her writing cave, she's spending time with her somewhat enormous but delightfully close family.

To the other authors who took part in this series:
Karen Templeton, Marie Ferrarella, Susan Crosby,
Nancy Robards Thompson and Allison Leigh.

Chapter One

Javier Mendoza might have been a little irritable and short-tempered with his family just moments ago, but all he really wanted was for them to go home and leave him alone.

When they finally got the hint and left his hospital room, he was relieved. That is, until they gathered out in the hall and began to whisper.

"Maybe it's time for us to call in a psychologist," his father said.

Luis Mendoza might have lowered his voice, thinking he couldn't be overheard, but Javier wasn't deaf.

He glanced at Leah Roberts, who stood at the foot of his bed. From the expression on his personal Florence Nightingale's pretty face, he realized the comments they'd both overheard had struck a sympathetic chord in her.

"They mean well," Leah said, her own voice lowering to a whisper so the family members who'd gathered in the hall couldn't hear her words.

She was right. His father and siblings had held prayer vigils while he'd been in the ICU and had continued to visit regularly, even after his condition had been upgraded and he'd been moved to a regular room. He was grateful for their love and concern, of course, but there wasn't anything wrong with his mental state. Dragging this whole thing out any longer than necessary wasn't going to get him back on his feet any sooner.

Two months ago, a tornado had struck Red Rock, and in the blink of an eye Javier's life had been permanently altered.

Of course, all he knew about that fateful day— and for the next three to four weeks after—was what others had told him and what he'd read in the old newspapers Leah had brought for him to read.

In fact, there was very little he recalled after the December day his brother Marcos had married Wendy Fortune. The two families had celebrated the Christmas holiday together, then the Atlanta-based Fortunes had planned to fly home to attend a New Year's Eve party.

It had taken several vehicles to deliver them all to the airport, and Javier had been one of the drivers.

The wind had kicked up and the clouds had grown dark, threatening to ground all the flights. So the travelers had hoped to get out of Red Rock before they were forced to wait out the storm.

Then the unthinkable happened. A tornado struck, killing several people and injuring others.

Javier, who'd almost gotten a one-way ticket to the Pearly Gates, had been one of the "lucky ones," which was what more than one medical professional had told him. In fact, his injuries had been so serious that it had been weeks before anyone knew if he'd pull through or not.

He supposed he had his family's prayers and the skill of one of the top neurosurgeons in the country to thank for that.

Still, he'd been in a coma for over a month, which had been medically induced for part of that time, and had finally regained consciousness in February.

His family and the many specialists who'd treated him had been relieved to learn he hadn't suffered any lasting brain damage, although he'd suffered a lot of confusion those first few days.

His recovery was going to be far from easy. He still faced some physical hurdles, since multiple fractures in both of his legs would require extensive rehab in the facility attached to the hospital, but at least he'd be able to walk again. For a while, doctors hadn't been sure.

Jeremy Fortune, Javier's orthopedic surgeon, as

well as a longtime family friend, had been honest about what the future would bring. The physical therapy would be grueling, but it was necessary for Javier to regain full body function.

"You're young," Jeremy had said. "And you're strong. With rehab, you'll eventually be as good as new."

But Javier wasn't convinced of that. He'd lost a lot of time, not to mention a once-in-a-lifetime business opportunity that had slipped through his fingers while he'd been out of commission. And thanks to the blasted confusion—which was better but still lingered—there'd been countless other details and opportunities lost to him.

Sure, the brain fog had cleared some, and with time, he'd probably regain his physical strength. But deep inside, where no one could see, something had changed.

Javier was different.

His family seemed to think he was depressed. Okay, so maybe he was—a little. Who wouldn't be?

For all of his thirty-one years, he'd relied on quick wit and keen business savvy to see him through. But after the injury and weeks of recovery, he feared the healing had stopped.

What if he never got his mental mojo back?

The question itself struck fear deep into his battered bones. And it was something he'd never admit to anyone, not even to a shrink.

Javier again looked at Leah, whose long, auburn hair was pulled back with a clip, whose expressive hazel eyes seemed to know what he was thinking and feeling most days without him ever having to say a word.

She was the only person whose presence didn't make him want to scream. Maybe that was because she hadn't known him before and didn't have any preconceived notions of how he "should" react to things. Or maybe he just appreciated the fact that she didn't walk on eggshells around him and act cheerful when she wasn't.

Then again, she was a beautiful woman, inside and out. How could he not want to be one hundred percent whenever he was around her? After all, he might be wounded, but he wasn't dead. And certain parts of his body weren't in need of any rehab at all.

Leah made her way to the head of his bed and rested her hand on the railing. Her fingers were long and tapered, her nails neatly manicured. Her touch, as he'd come to expect, was light yet steady and competent.

He was tempted to reach out to her, to place his hand over hers. But before he could ponder the wisdom—or the repercussions—of doing so, she said, "I'll ask them to continue their discussion in one of the conference rooms."

That would help. "Thanks."

She nodded, then left his room to join his family in the hall.

The last voice he heard was Leah's saying, "Why don't you come with me."

As Leah led the Mendoza family past the nurses' station, their footsteps clicking upon the tile floor, she said, "Javier was listening to your conversation, so I thought it would be best if you finished your discussion in private."

"Aw, man." Luis, Javier's dad, raked a hand through his hair. "I didn't mean for him to overhear what we were saying. It's just that we've been worried about him."

Leah had been concerned, too. She'd noticed the change in Javier's attitude whenever his family came to visit. She'd even asked him about it one day, although he'd shrugged it off as no big deal and then changed the subject.

"Being incapacitated is a big blow to a man like him," Leah said as she walked along the hall.

They all nodded in agreement.

"It's too bad you didn't know him before he was injured," Luis said.

Leah would have liked knowing him before. Even in his injured condition, she'd found him to be intriguing. And if truth be told, she stopped by to visit him even on those days when she'd been assigned to other rooms and patients.

"Javier is a contractor and a real estate developer," Luis added as he strode next to Leah. "And he's always been enthusiastic about whatever project he was working on. In fact, those deals always seemed to energize him. But now, if we mention anything about business or properties, he changes the subject."

Leah had picked up quite a few details about her patient, including the fact that he'd been very successful with his land dealings and that he had a nice house in one of the better areas of Red Rock—custom-built just for him.

"He's also a part-time musician," Isabella, his older sister, added. "And he's an athlete. He played both tennis and golf before his accident. But if we mention music or sports, he clamps his lips tight and his expression turns grim."

"I'm sure, in time, he'll play golf and tennis again." Leah opened the door of the conference room that was located just beyond the nurses' station and waited for Luis Mendoza to enter, followed by his son, Rafe. Next came Rafe's wife, Melina, and Isabella.

"My brother has always been positive and energetic," Isabella said. "So it's heartbreaking to see him depressed."

"I'm sure it is." From everything Leah had gathered, Javier Mendoza was bright, ambitious and successful. She'd also overheard his family mention that he had an active social life and that he was one of Red Rock's most eligible bachelors.

To be honest, if Leah had run into him before the accident—and if he'd given her the time of day—she would have found him more than a little appealing herself.

Actually, she did now—even when he was stretched out on a hospital bed or seated in a wheelchair.

"I'm an occupational therapist," Melina said. "So I understand where Javier is coming from. I've worked with many accident victims, some of whom had to face the reality of never being the men or women they once were. It's tough to face your own mortality and frailties, so Javier's depression is only natural. Besides, he's a competitor at heart. And he's always prided himself on being the best. So dealing with his incapacitation—even one that's temporary—is going to be especially tough for him."

"That's what I'm talking about." Luis looked at Leah as though appealing for her agreement. "Don't you think it would be good if he talked to a psychologist or a counselor?"

"Yes, I do," she admitted. "And once he's moved into a room at the rehab facility, he'll have an opportunity to speak to a professional."

"So you're saying we should back off?" Luis asked.

If there's one thing Leah had learned about Javier Mendoza, it was that he didn't like to be pushed—whether it was to eat a bit more of his meal or to take some medication to help him sleep.

"I would wait a bit longer," she said. "He has a lot to deal with right now. Time is really your best ally."

The family seemed to ponder her suggestion, which she hoped was the right one. When Dr. Fortune ordered Javier's transfer to the rehab unit, she'd be sure to mention the family's concern in her report.

"You know," Rafe said, "I've been thinking. We've asked his friends and business associates to refrain from coming to see him. After all, he was in a drug-induced coma for a month. And then they brought him out of it slowly. For a while, he suffered some confusion, so we knew he wouldn't want to see anyone other than family. But maybe it's time to let people know that he'd like to have visitors."

"I don't know about that," Isabella said. "His mood is difficult enough for *us* to deal with."

"I'm not saying that we should encourage *everyone* to visit, but what about one of those women he used to date?" Rafe reached for Melina's hand. "My lady always puts a smile on my face."

At that, everyone in the room broke into a grin.

Everyone except Leah.

Somehow, she didn't like to think of the women Javier used to date before his injury and hospitalization. And why was that?

It wasn't as though she had plans to date him herself. She'd never get involved with one of her patients.

Oh, no? a small inner voice asked. Then why did

her heart drop each time she saw that Javier's room had been assigned to another nurse?

She didn't have an answer to that—only to argue that she'd grown fond of Javier. She understood the uphill battle he'd been waging and seemed to have bonded with him somehow.

The fact that he was not only handsome, but personable, and that she found him attractive had nothing to do with it.

That's not true, that pesky little voice said.

As much as she wanted to object, to defend herself and her feelings, she had to admit that there was something about Javier Mendoza that called to her.

Something she couldn't explain.

Javier had been surfing the channels on the television in his hospital room for several minutes, but he couldn't seem to find any shows that interested him.

A tennis match only made him resent the fact that he wouldn't be able to play for months, if not years. And the news stations reminded him of how much he'd missed during the time he'd spent in the ICU.

Hell, he could hardly remember what his life had been like outside these white walls, and as he thought of his hospitalization and the long road to recovery, frustration swooped down on him again like a hungry vulture unable to wait for his hope to completely expire.

With the dark shadow came the urge to throw the

remote across the room, even though he'd never been prone to displays of temper. Instead, he placed his index finger over the red power button, shutting off the TV.

As the screen faded to black, Leah entered the room. Just the sight of his pretty nurse was enough to make his frustration ease and his mood take flight.

Talk about a nice diversion…

A grin tugged at his lips, softening what had been a grimace only moments ago.

At first glance, Leah, who stood about five foot four, wasn't what Javier would call a striking woman. After all, he'd never seen her wearing anything other than hospital scrubs and a matching pair of Crocs on her feet. But with each passing day, as he looked beyond the loose-fitting clothing that masked her femininity, he'd found a lot to admire.

Her long, straight hair was a pretty shade of auburn, although she usually kept it pulled back with a clip or woven in a single braid. She wore very little makeup—if any. But she had such a wholesome beauty that she really didn't need any of the usual female props.

He wondered what she looked like on her days off or when she spent a night on the town. In fact, he'd like to know a lot of things about her, like what her life was like outside the hospital.

Was she married?

He certainly hoped not.

As she moved through his room, he wondered if she was dating someone special. It was difficult to imagine men not clamoring to be her one and only. How many women were as comforting, as gentle, as sweet?

A couple of times he'd been tempted to ask if she was single and unattached, but he hadn't, and he wasn't sure why. He supposed he hadn't wanted his nurse to know that he found her that attractive. If he hadn't been laid up—and barely able to walk—it might be a different story. In fact, the old Javier wouldn't have thought twice about asking her out. But he was a far cry from the man he used to be.

"I take it there's nothing good on television," she said.

"Nope." He set the remote aside.

"The dinner cart will be here shortly," she added.

"I can hardly wait."

Catching his sarcastic tone, she turned to him and smiled. "You're lucky. The food at San Antonio General is actually pretty good."

Maybe it was, but his appetite had yet to return. In fact, the only reason he even looked forward to mealtime was because it helped to pass the time from morning to night, making him come one day closer to discharge.

But why focus on all that mundane reality when he had Leah with him?

"Hey, Florence," he said, using the nickname he'd

dubbed her with when he'd first began to see her as a woman and not as his nurse. "I have a question for you."

"What's that?" She neared his bed, checking the ice and water level in the small plastic pitcher that sat on his portable tray.

"What does your husband do for a living? Is he in the medical field, too?"

She paused as if his comment had thrown her for a loop. "My *husband?* I'm not married."

Javier fought the urge to smile at that news. "Oh, no? I just assumed that a woman like you would have a man in her life."

Her hand lifted to the boxy pink top she wore and she fingered the stitching along the V-neck.

Was she nervous? Off balance? Flattered maybe?

He liked to think so, even though he wasn't in a position to follow through at this point.

Before either of them could speak, a woman's voice sounded in the doorway.

At the cheery "Hello," both Javier and Leah turned to see a tall, willowy blonde walk into the room carrying an arrangement of spring flowers that hid her face.

Savannah Bennett?

As the blonde lowered the multicolored blooms, he realized that's exactly who'd come to visit.

"I hope you don't mind me stopping by," Savannah said. "I'd been wanting to see you for weeks, but

I'd heard that your visitors had been limited to family members."

No one had told Javier that only his relatives were allowed to see him, although he hadn't much cared either way. In fact, he'd rather not deal with visitors at all—whether they be family or friends.

"But then I ran into Rafe at the grocery store this afternoon," Savannah said. "He told me you were eager to have company. So here I am."

Eager? That was a crock, and Rafe knew it.

More irritated at his brother's interference than Savannah's surprise visit, he forced himself to be polite. "Thanks for stopping by."

He wondered if Savannah noticed that his tone lacked sincerity. After all, they hadn't dated in a couple of months—well, make that four or five, since they'd split up way before the tornado had struck Red Rock.

Savannah had wanted more from him than he'd been able to give her—like a commitment. And while he'd made no bones about being a happy bachelor, she seemed to think that she was the one woman who would eventually change his mind. So there'd been a few tears on her part, but he'd suspected she would have been a lot more hurt and disappointed if he'd strung her along.

Of course, Rafe had no way of knowing any of that. Javier had never been one to kiss and tell—or to break up and vent.

Leah, who'd been standing by his bed, took a step back, as though trying to bow out graciously.

She wasn't going to leave him alone with Savannah, was she? Not that it mattered, he supposed. It's just that he... Well, he didn't want Leah to go. Not when she provided the only upbeat moments in his day.

"Hey, Florence," he said, trying to recapture the playful moment they'd been having—or that they'd been about to have before Savannah's arrival.

Leah paused, her expression unreadable. "Yes?"

For a moment he was at a loss for words. But he wanted to let both women know he and the blonde weren't romantically involved, at least not any longer.

"I'd like to introduce you to a friend of mine," he told his nurse. "Savannah's a paralegal at a local law firm. Or she was, the last time we talked." He turned to his unexpected visitor. "Are you still working for Higgins and Lamphier?"

Savannah nodded, her demeanor a bit stiff and a frown creasing her brow.

"It's nice to meet you," Leah said with a casual smile. Then she nodded toward the doorway. "I'd better get back to work and let you two chat."

Javier could have argued, asked her not to leave. But then what? His obvious attraction to his nurse would have only complicated any future discussion he had with Savannah.

And his life was complicated enough as it was.

Chapter Two

As Leah slipped into the hall, a whisper of uneasiness breezed through her. She could have sworn that Javier had been about to ask whether she was single and maybe even...

Available?

Okay. So maybe she'd only imagined that's what he'd been getting at.

When it came right down to it, she wasn't sure why he'd asked those questions or what he'd meant by them. The minute Savannah what's-her-name had entered the room, their conversation had ended before it even had a chance to take off, so all bets were off.

And really, wasn't she better off not knowing what Javier had planned to say next? The last thing she needed to do was to create any unnecessary workday drama.

Still, the line of questioning had taken her aback and made her face the fact that, in spite of her efforts to remain completely professional, she was growing a little too fond of one of her patients.

Of course, she would never act on her attraction. She was too committed to her job to let anything like that get out of hand.

As she made her way to the nurses' station, glad to be back on the job and out of Javier's room, she held her head high, her shoulders straight. Yet disappointment threatened to drag her down for the count. She was sorry about the way things had played out.

And why was that? she wondered.

Probably because she cared more for her patient than she should. So for that reason alone she really ought to be glad that Savannah's arrival had interrupted their conversation.

And she *was*.

Yet she'd flinched when the beautiful blonde had entered Javier's room, and she'd found her emotional reaction to the visit more than a little bothersome. After all, Javier was a handsome bachelor. He probably had a slew of women in his pre-hospital life. How could he not?

So why would one woman's visit surprise her? And why would it leave her so unsettled, so uneasy?

She supposed that was because, at least up until

now, only his family had come to see him. And she hadn't given his love life much thought.

Well, now...that wasn't entirely true. She'd thought about the women he might have dated in the past, but in all of her musings they'd been faceless beauties.

Of course, that was no longer the case. Now one of them had a face—a pretty one that suggested Javier liked tall, sophisticated blondes who dressed to the nines and were skilled at applying makeup and styling their own hair.

Leah clicked her tongue, scolding herself for making that kind of assumption. Maybe she was connecting all the wrong dots. How did she know that Savannah and Javier had actually dated? Hadn't he downplayed that possibility?

If he had no idea whether she still held the same job, how could he and Savannah be romantically involved? Clearly, he hadn't seen her in a while.

Leah's uneasiness began to lift at that conclusion—until she realized he'd spent more than two months in the hospital. He'd also been in a coma for nearly half that time. And he'd suffered some confusion and memory loss when he'd first come to.

Then, to make matters worse, she remembered what his brother Rafe had suggested to the family earlier this morning.

So it was easy to conclude that Savannah's hospital visit hadn't been a coincidence. In fact, Rafe had set it into motion when he'd run into her at the grocery store earlier today.

It hadn't taken much of a leap for Leah to realize that, even if Javier had made it sound as if he and Savannah were merely friends, that hadn't always been the case. At one time, they must have been more involved than that.

As Leah took a seat behind the desk, she had to admit that she didn't like the idea of Javier having a girlfriend, which meant that her feelings had grown to the point that they bordered on that fine line between sympathetic and inappropriate.

Bordered? She was afraid that she might have crossed the line already, and that she was more attracted to her patient than a nurse ought to be.

So the way she saw it, she would either have to request a transfer to another floor or fight her feelings so she wouldn't compromise her professional ethics.

With the dilemma still weighing on her mind, she reached for a chart belonging to another of her patients and tried to pretend she was busy. Yet even though she studied the paperwork in front of her, her thoughts were a million miles away.

Okay, so they weren't all that far away. They were just down the hall, with Javier and the attractive blonde who'd come to visit him. A frown slowly stretched across her face as she realized she had no one to blame for her green-eyed uneasiness but herself.

For some reason, while he'd been on the third floor at San Antonio General, she'd come to think of him as...

Well, unattached, she supposed. And even pondering his romantic status had been the first hint that her interest in him was out of line.

So now what? Should she request a transfer to either the obstetric or pediatric ward? That might help.

Trouble was, Javier's mood lifted whenever she was around. And Margie Graybill, who worked the night shift, had told his family that Javier never cracked a smile, no matter how hard she tried to coax one out of him.

"You must have a special touch," Javier's father had said to Leah the other day. "His attitude is much better whenever you're on duty."

She liked to think that she had managed to reach him when other nurses hadn't. So if she was one of a few who had the ability to draw him out of his somber mood, how could she ask for a transfer?

What kind of nurse would she be if she gave up on her patient when he needed her most?

Leah had lucked out. She'd finished the rest of her shift without having to go back into Javier's room. But that didn't mean she wasn't aware of who went in or came out.

Savannah had left the hospital shortly after she'd

arrived, which had pleased Leah more than it should have, especially since she'd made up her mind to maintain a professional attitude when it came to Javier. But there wasn't anything remotely professional about the rush of relief she'd felt when the blonde had left his room after only a few minutes— five or six at the most.

Leah glanced at her wristwatch, realizing it was about time for the shift change. Thank goodness she didn't have to work tomorrow. Taking a break from her handsome patient would help tremendously. She'd shake those inappropriate thoughts and feelings that surfaced whenever she was near him.

As she opened the last patient's chart and prepared to make a note before leaving the hospital for the next couple of days, Leanne Beattie, the nurse's aide who delivered meals to the third floor, said, "The guy in three-fourteen doesn't seem to like anything we serve him."

The guy in 314 was Javier.

Leah glanced up from the note she was writing, "What do you mean?"

"Well, he hasn't eaten much of anything today. He didn't touch his breakfast and only picked at his lunch. As far as I can tell, he left everything except the chocolate ice cream on his dinner tray. So I thought I should mention it."

"Thanks, Leanne. Loss of appetite is a side effect

of one of the new medications he's on, so I'll be sure to tell his doctor."

Of course, the depression his family had been concerned about might also contribute to him not eating, although Leah wasn't convinced that they were right. Whatever was bothering him only seemed to flare up when he had visitors.

But either way, she'd like to see him start eating better. He was going to need his strength when he moved to the rehab unit and his physical therapy became more vigorous than it was now.

On her drive home that night, she thought about her own dinner and what she'd like to eat. For the most part, she avoided red meat, fats and processed foods. But she'd had the munchies ever since she'd left Savannah and Javier alone in his room, so she decided to give in to temptation and pick up a cheeseburger and fries.

She didn't allow herself those kinds of indulgences very often, but she figured the fast food would be filling—and it was better than fixing herself a salad with low-fat dressing, then popping open the freezer and wolfing down the rest of a carton of rocky road ice cream, which was what she'd probably end up doing when the veggies didn't hit the spot.

And on a night like this, she didn't think a salad was going to be enough to hold back temptation.

As she pulled into the drive-through of her favorite fast-food restaurant, she realized that people sometimes craved foods that they'd grown up eating. There were days when nothing else would do the trick.

At that thought, a game plan began to unfold.

She didn't have to work tomorrow. Why not take lunch to Javier? She could pick up something tasty that was a change from the usual hospital fare he'd been served. Maybe that would spark his appetite and entice him to eat a full meal.

So the next morning, after cleaning her small apartment, she took a shower and slipped into her favorite jeans and the new black sweater Aunt Connie had given her for her birthday. Then, after applying a little makeup, brushing out her hair and pulling it back in a ponytail, she drove to the most popular Mexican restaurant in Red Rock, which Jose and Maria Mendoza owned.

Jose was related to Javier's father, Luis, although Leah wasn't entirely sure of the exact connection. They might be cousins, she supposed. Either way, it was probably safe to assume the entire Mendoza clan spent a good deal of time eating at Red.

Actually, she was surprised that none of Javier's relatives had come up with the idea before. But she wouldn't think about that now. Instead, she would surprise him by taking him lunch.

At a few minutes after eleven, Leah arrived at Red and parked her car out front. So far, not many people had gathered, but she knew it was only a matter of time before the lunch crowd would begin to roll in.

She'd only eaten at the restaurant once before, and that was several years ago. But she'd been impressed by the historic building, which had once been a hacienda.

The Mendozas had done a great job decorating with nineteenth-century photographs, antiques and Southwestern artwork that lined the walls.

In fact, while waiting for her order to be prepared, she might even sit in the courtyard, with its rustic old fountain, lush plants and the colorful umbrellas that shaded pine tables and chairs. There she'd listen to the soft sounds of mariachi music coming from the lounge, as well as the relaxing gurgle of the water in the fountain while sitting amidst the bougainvillea that bloomed in shades of fuchsia, purple and gold.

As Leah entered the door, a dark-haired hostess greeted her. "One for lunch? Or are you meeting someone?"

"Actually, I'd like to place an order to go."

The woman reached for a menu. "Do you already know what you'd like? Or would you like to see what we have to offer?"

Leah took the menu. "I'll need a moment or two to decide. But can you tell me if Marcos Mendoza is here today?"

Javier's brother managed the restaurant. And if anyone knew what Leah should order, it would be him.

"Yes, Marcos is here. I think he's in the kitchen. I'll get him for you."

From what Leah had heard, Marcos used to spend a great deal of time at Red, making sure that everything ran smoothly. But he actually kept a regular schedule now that he and Wendy had a new baby. Their little girl, who had been born a month early but was doing well now, was expected to be released from the neonatal intensive care unit soon.

Leah knew all this because she'd taken to stopping by the NICU to see Mary Anne Mendoza and the other preemies...and wondering what it would be like to have a baby of her own.

Sure, the neonatal unit housed the most seriously ill newborns, but while some didn't make it, many of them did. And as a nurse she was proud of the success rate.

In fact, each year, the NICU staff put on a reunion party for the children who'd once been patients and who'd gone home healthy. The oldest were about ten years old now, and some of the parents had created play groups that were still going strong.

While waiting for Javier's brother, Leah opened the menu and studied her options. Marcos might know what Javier would like to eat, but she planned to choose something for herself.

Who knew what might happen when she surprised him with his favorite Mexican meal. He might even ask her to join him for lunch. And if he did? She'd agree. Otherwise, she'd take her food home and eat it there.

"Can I help you?" Marcos asked upon his approach.

When she looked up from the menu and smiled, recognition dawned on his face. "What a surprise, Leah. I didn't realize who you were in street clothes."

"That's not surprising. I practically live in scrubs."

"How are things going?" Marcos asked. "I didn't get a chance to stop by and see my brother last night. Wendy and I wanted to talk to the neonatologist when he made his morning rounds, so I had to work late to make up for being gone."

Wendy, who'd once worked at Red, too, had been expecting a baby this month, but she'd gone into premature labor back in January. The doctors had managed to stave off her contractions, then they'd put her on bed rest. She'd eventually given birth at home in early February, which had to be a real worry for them. But the baby girl was small but healthy and now thriving.

At least, that's the last Leah had heard. "Mary Anne's still doing okay, isn't she?"

"Yes, everything is great. She's been gaining weight, and the doctor is pleased with her progress." A broad smile told Leah that the new father couldn't be happier.

"I'm glad to hear that," she said.

"It was a little scary for a while," Marcos admitted, "but we're all doing great. In fact, now that Mary Anne is out of the woods, Wendy and I are settling into parenthood. We've even been thinking about having a party soon to celebrate our daughter's birth."

With the size of the Fortune and Mendoza families, that would probably be some party. And Leah couldn't help but smile.

The two families had been through a lot lately, first with the tornado and Javier's injury, then with Wendy's baby. So now that everyone was on the road to health and wellness, they had a lot to celebrate.

"The hostess said you wanted to talk to me," Marcos said. "Is everything all right?"

He was worried about Javier, Leah realized, so she shot him a smile to put his mind at ease. "Your brother is coming along just fine, but I have a feeling that he's getting tired of the hospital food. So I thought I'd surprise him with something different for a change. Do you have any suggestions? What does he usually order when he comes here?"

Marcos chuckled. "I don't suppose they'd let you sneak him an ice-cold beer and lime."

"I'm afraid not," Leah said, enjoying the brotherly humor.

"Well, he'll be happy with the carne asada, which is what he usually orders."

"Then I'll take a plate to go."

"How about you?" Marcos asked. "Aren't you going to have lunch with him?"

The thought had certainly crossed Leah's mind, but she wasn't so sure it was a good idea any longer.

Marcos must have read her indecision, because he added, "My brother seems to really like you, and I'm sure he'll be more likely to enjoy his meal if you share it with him."

He had a point, she supposed. "All right. I'll take the small chicken taco salad."

She reached into her purse.

"Oh, no you don't," Marcos said, placing a hand on her arm. "Put your money away. After all you've done for Javier, this order is on the house."

She wanted to object, to tell him she'd just been doing her job, that she'd fully intended to pay for lunch, that she hadn't chosen the family's restaurant hoping to get a freebie. But both appreciation and sincerity lit up his smile, so she released her wallet and thanked him instead.

"Is there anything else you need? Dessert maybe? Javier likes the flan. I can also pack up napkins, silverware—whatever else you might need."

She was going to say that the takeout order was enough, then another idea struck. A *good* one.

"You know," she said, "I just might need a little more help from you after all."

When she told Marcos what she had in mind, he grinned and nodded his head in agreement. Then he turned to the hostess. "Give her whatever she wants."

Five minutes later, as Leah waited for her order, she went into the courtyard to cut a few sprigs of the fuchsia-colored bougainvillea with the scissors the hostess had given her.

As she took the last cutting, she wondered how Javier would react to her surprise.

The man was a little moody at times and hard to read, so it was anyone's guess. But the idea had certainly put a bounce in her step and a smile on her face. She just hoped it did the same for him.

Javier had just talked to Jeremy Fortune, who'd told him he'd be sending him to the rehab unit tomorrow or the next day, depending upon when they had a bed available.

"You won't have to stay very long," Jeremy added. "After you're discharged, you can do the rest of your rehab as an outpatient."

"That's the best news I've had in months." Javier blew out a weary sigh, glad to see some light at the end of the tunnel, even if he still had a long road to full recovery and a life he'd have to recreate in many ways. "You have no idea how badly I want to get out of here."

"I can imagine." Jeremy placed a hand on Javier's shoulder. "You've been through a lot these past two months. In fact, if you ever feel the need to talk to a professional, I can refer you to someone."

Javier stiffened and clucked his tongue. "Did my family put you up to that?"

"No, they didn't. Do they think you need counseling?"

"It was suggested," Javier admitted, before making his own opinion clear. "But I *don't* need it."

"I'm not saying that you do. Just know that it's available should you change your mind. And that if you do decide to talk to someone, it wouldn't be a sign of weakness."

Maybe not, but Javier already felt like a ninety-pound weakling going up against a UFC fighter in a championship bout, and that's what frustrated the hell out of him.

Still, Jeremy had a point—and Javier knew that his family had reason to be concerned, too.

"Well, I've still got several patients yet to see," Jeremy said, "so I'd better finish my rounds."

"I...uh..." Javier heaved another sigh. "I'm sorry, Doc."

"What for?" Jeremy asked.

"For snapping at you." Javier ran his hand through his hair, which was shorter than he was used to, thanks to the neurosurgery he'd had two months back. "I've been pretty quick-tempered lately, and you don't deserve to be the target of my frustration."

Of course, neither did his family. Maybe he really *should* talk to a counselor, someone he could unload on instead of the people who loved him the most.

"Don't worry about it," Jeremy said. "You've got every reason to be irritable. You nearly died, spent a month of your life in a coma, woke up in pain and confusion. And now that you're facing some intensive physical therapy… It's enough to make anyone touchy."

Yeah, well maybe Javier had better figure out a way to shake that dark cloud that hovered over him. His future might be messed up, but he didn't need to make everyone else's life miserable, too.

"I'll see you tomorrow," Jeremy said as he turned to go. Then he stopped in his tracks, allowing someone to enter the room.

But not just any someone. It was Leah.

What was she doing here? She was supposed to be off today.

She was definitely not on the clock since she was wearing regular clothes—a black sweater and jeans. Her glossy auburn hair had been pulled back in a soft, loose ponytail.

She'd draped a striped, brightly colored serape over her shoulder. What was she doing with a Mexican blanket that looked a lot like one his sister Isabella might have woven?

Leah greeted Jeremy first. "Hello, Dr. Fortune."

"Do you need any help?" he asked. "It looks like you've got a full load."

That was for sure. In one hand, she held a heat-insulated bag with the familiar Red logo, and in the other, she held a couple of sprigs of bougainvillea.

"Thanks for the offer, Doctor. But I've got everything balanced just right."

As she placed the insulated bag on the chair near Javier's bed, Jeremy stepped out of the hospital room and into the hall, leaving the two of them alone.

"What's all this?" Javier asked.

"I decided to surprise you with a picnic."

In the hospital? Was she kidding?

"I would have taken you out into the rose garden in a wheelchair," she added, "but I figured this was better for now."

"What's in the bag?"

"Carne asada, rice, beans, chips, salsa, guacamole... And a taco salad for me."

Javier didn't know what to say. Nor could he get over the sight of her in a form-fitting sweater and a pair of tight jeans, rather than those blousy hospital scrubs he was used to seeing her wear. More than once he'd tried to imagine what she hid behind the loose-fitting fabric, but now...?

Dang. There wasn't much need to guess. Denim didn't lie. At least, hers certainly didn't.

She draped the serape over the portable bed table. Next, she pulled out a small vase and filled it with a couple of sprigs of the bougainvillea that he suspected she'd found growing in one of the clay pots in the courtyard of his family's restaurant. Then she placed it on top of the serape-covered table.

For a moment, he almost forgot that he was in a hospital—and that he'd been there for ages.

He nodded toward the Cinco-de-Mayo-style decorations. "That's a nice touch."

"I thought so." Her smile nearly turned him inside out. He'd always considered her attractive when she'd tended him as his nurse, but now?

His head was almost spinning as he tried to take it all in, tried to take *her* all in. He'd never seen hair that color—a rusty shade of auburn—and wondered if she ever wore it loose and wild.

He'd only seen it pulled back and out of her face, but he could imagine it splayed across a white pillow…

Cut it out, he told himself. Thoughts like that weren't going to do him any good in a place like this.

He was tempted to call her Florence, to try and put some lighthearted humor into the situation, but all he could think of was one of the oldies but goodies his dad used to play on the radio in the car. "Just look at her in those blue jeans, her hair in a pony tail."

She could be Venus, as far as he was concerned.

He hadn't even been alive when that song had first come out, but he was tempted to hum the tune or even belt out the lyrics—something he'd been known to do when the mood struck him.

And it was the first time the mood had struck him since last Christmas Eve, when he'd sung "Grandma

Got Run Over by a Reindeer" just to make the kids laugh.

"I hope you don't mind me bringing lunch," Leah said.

"Not at all." Heck, right now, he didn't care if she poked him with a hypodermic needle. "It was a really nice thing for you to do. Thanks for thinking of me."

How many nurses went above and beyond the call of duty like that?

He reached for the button that lifted the head of his bed higher, then adjusted the pillows so that he was sitting up.

As Leah removed the food from the red bag, he caught a whiff of beef and spices, of cilantro and chili, and his stomach actually growled.

"This is going to be some picnic," he said as his eyes scanned the food she set out on the serape-covered table.

"Eating outdoors would have been nice," she said. "But look at it this way, at least we don't need to worry about avoiding ants or using sunblock."

"You've got a point there."

Moments later, with the table set, she pulled up a chair to sit beside his bed and they began to eat.

Javier stuck his fork into a piece of marinated beef and popped it into his mouth.

Dang. When was the last time he'd tasted meat so tender, so tasty?

After relishing another bite, he said, "I can't tell

you how much I appreciate this. How'd you come up with an idea like this?"

"It just struck me on the way home last night. You've been eating at the hospital for weeks on end, and while I think the food is pretty good, I can see where you might get tired of it."

He'd gotten tired of just about everything in the hospital. Everything except his nurse.

"I asked Marcos which meal was your favorite," she said, "and he suggested the carne asada. Would you have preferred the chile rellenos? Or maybe the tamales? He said you liked them, too."

"No, this is perfect. If I'm still in this room tomorrow, maybe I can have someone at Red deliver us another meal. I owe you one now."

"You don't owe me anything."

That's not the way he saw it. If not for Leah, he might have gone stir-crazy weeks ago.

They finished their meals in silence, but that didn't mean Javier's mind wasn't going a jillion miles an hour—plotting and planning—much like it used to do before the injury.

Finally he said, "I'm going to be transferred to the rehab unit within the next couple of days."

She paused, her fork in midmotion. Her pretty eyes, a whiskey shade of hazel, widened. Then she smiled. "That's good news. You're getting closer to being able to go home. I bet you can't wait."

He wanted to leave the hospital; that was a given.

But he wasn't keen on the idea of never seeing Leah again.

Why had she done all of this for him? And on her day off?

He could read all kinds of things into her effort to surprise him, he supposed. But he wouldn't. Instead, he planned to enjoy the meal and the nurse who'd brought a bit of sunshine on a mundane day, the beautiful Florence Nightingale who'd provided him with a taste of the real world he was about to reenter.

Chapter Three

The next morning, while Dr. Fortune was making his rounds, Javier learned that he would be transferred to the rehab unit within the next hour or so.

After two long months, he would finally put that devastating, life-altering tragedy behind him. But leaving the third floor also meant leaving Leah.

He supposed he could always look her up after he was discharged from the hospital completely, but not until he was back on his feet and had a better grip on just who the post-tornado Javier really was—and where his future lay.

Still, he hoped to see her before he left, to say goodbye, to talk one last time. But he might not get the chance since Karen, one of the other third-floor nurses, had already come in and told him she'd been assigned to his room for the day.

Karen was nice enough, but she wasn't…

Well, she wasn't Leah.

Javier had just turned on the television to watch the midday news when his dad, Rafe and Isabella entered his room.

Determined to be a little more upbeat and better tempered than he'd been in the past, he greeted them, then reached for the remote and shut off the power to the TV.

"How's it going?" his dad asked.

Javier gave them the good news that he was moving to rehab, which meant he was one step closer to being discharged and sent home.

"That's great," Isabella said.

Rafe and his father broke into smiles, too, clearly in agreement. Then his dad pointed toward the serape that was now draped over the back of the chair by his bed. "What's that doing here?"

Javier smiled, thinking about the lunch he'd shared with Leah. "I had a surprise visitor yesterday and she brought that to me, along with some carne asada, which beat the heck out of what I've been eating."

"So Savannah came by to see you," Rafe said with a grin—no doubt pleased with himself for setting it all up.

"Yes, she came by. And she gave me those flowers by the window. But Leah's the one who brought the serape and the food I hadn't realized I'd been craving."

"That was nice of her," Luis said. "The entire nursing staff has been great, but I gotta admit, Leah's one of my favorites."

She was one of Javier's, too.

"When will they transfer you to your new room?" Isabella asked.

"Probably within the next hour." Javier studied his sister, with her long brown hair and big brown eyes. She was actually his half sister, a young woman he'd only met seven years ago.

Javier's father had married young and divorced shortly thereafter. He'd been very involved in Isabella's life, but when his ex-wife remarried and relocated to California, she took Isabella with her and disappeared under the radar for more than fifteen years.

Javier's dad had been devastated to lose contact with his daughter, and even after he married Elena, Javier's mom, and started a new family, he'd never forgotten his "little girl."

When Javier was born, Luis had been thrilled to have a son. Yet he hadn't made a secret of the fact that he would never truly be happy until Isabella was found.

Javier and his brothers knew they were loved, of course. And that they each had a secure position in the family. Still Javier had always gone out of his way to make his father proud and to fill the hole in his heart created by Isabella's loss.

Deep inside, Javier had hoped that his achievements would enable his dad to forget Isabella and to get on with his life.

Of course, Luis had always been incredibly proud of Javier—of all his sons, for that matter. But he'd never forgotten his firstborn or given up hope that they'd be reconciled someday.

By the time Javier finally understood the depth of his father's love for *all* his children, the need to win and come out on top had become so ingrained in his character that Isabella's memory no longer had anything to do with it.

When Isabella finally reached adulthood and found Luis, the entire family welcomed her with open arms, including Javier, who actually liked having a big sister, especially one who was as artistic and talented as she was sweet. And he couldn't imagine what their lives would have been like if she'd never come back home to San Antonio.

Isabella, who'd married J. R. Fortune a few years back, was a talented Tejana craftswoman, as well as an interior designer. So it wasn't a surprise that the handwoven blanket had caught her interest.

"That's amazing." Isabella made her way to the chair and lifted the serape, carefully looking it over. "This is one of mine. Where did Leah find it?"

"I don't know. My guess is that Marcos gave it to

her when she was at Red. She brought that vase and the bougainvillea, too."

If anyone thought the nurse had gone above and beyond, they didn't say it, and Javier was glad. He'd been doing a little too much thinking about what might or might not be going on between the two of them as it was.

"I'll have to ask Leah about it when I see her," Isabella said. "Is she working today?"

"I think so, but I haven't seen her yet."

Javier and his family made small talk for a while, and he did his best to act interested in everything they had to say, especially about what was going on outside the hospital walls. Since he could finally see some light at the end of the tunnel, he was going to have to play catch-up if he was ever going to recreate—or, more likely, reinvent—his life.

Just as his family was saying their goodbyes, Leah entered his room.

She wore a pair of light blue scrubs today, so she was obviously working. And the fact that she'd made the effort to stop by to see him, especially when she didn't have to, brought a smile to his lips.

The Mendozas greeted her, then excused themselves and headed for the door.

When they were gone, Leah said, "You have a nice family. They're so loving and supportive."

Javier merely nodded his agreement.

"I've noticed that you're not always happy to see them," Leah added.

A stab of guilt robbed him of his smile. "It's not that I'm unhappy when they stop by."

"Then what is it? Do you have issues with them?"

"No, it's just that… I don't know. I guess you could say that I feel as though I've failed them somehow."

"How? I don't understand."

By not being at the top of his game…

By being flawed and less than perfect…

By him needing their help instead of it being the other way around…

Javier had always been the one to step up to the plate, the one who'd had money to loan, advice to give, but he didn't feel like admitting any of those things. Instead, he said, "I guess it's their sympathetic expressions that bother me. Sometimes, I wanted to climb the walls—and probably would have, if I could have gotten out of the damn bed."

"They love you, Javier. You can't blame them for being worried about you. First because they thought they would lose you, and now because they sense you're wrestling with something."

She was right on all counts, he supposed. But how did he admit that the struggle was in the realization that he was less than the best—something he wasn't sure he'd ever get used to?

Competition and winning had always come easily for him, whether it was in academics, sports, business…or even romance. But now he wasn't anywhere near as confident about anything, and that bothered him more than he cared to admit to anyone—even to Leah.

"Your family would like to help," she said. "But they can't unless you let them."

He hated feeling helpless, something he'd felt ever since regaining consciousness. But instead of making that admission, he said, "Some roads are meant to be traveled alone."

Leah eased closer to his bed and placed her hand on his arm. "Most of the time, it's nice to have someone at your side or in your corner."

Their gazes met and locked. For a moment, he wondered if she was offering *her* support even though he was about to leave her care. But before he could make any real assumptions, she withdrew her hand and took a step back, as if she'd realized that she'd overstepped her boundaries.

And maybe she had. Javier wasn't up for a relationship until he was back on top, and God only knew when that would be.

While the patients ate lunch and Leah manned the nurses' station, the call Javier had been waiting for finally came in. An orderly was on the way to get him and take him to the rehab unit.

Leah hated to see him go, but it was really for the

best. Hopefully, she'd find the old saying to be true—
out of sight, out of mind.

She took some comfort in that thought until another old adage came to mind. What if absence made
the heart grow fonder?

At that possibility, she clucked her tongue, then
told herself no. Once Javier was gone, she was determined to put him out of her mind and to focus on her
work and the other patients.

Still, she was glad that she would be the one to give
him the news that an orderly was coming to get him,
even though it was Karen's job to do that today. But
Karen had taken an early lunch break and Leah was
covering for her.

So she turned to Brenna, the LVN who was working at the desk with her. "I'm going to step away for
a minute or two. Will you get the phone if it rings?"

When Brenna agreed, Leah went to Javier's room,
where she found him wearing a grimace as he carefully set aside a pair of crutches he'd been using for
balance and then climbed back into bed. Earlier in the
week, Dr. Fortune had surgically removed several of
the pins that had held his broken bones in place until
they healed, leaving some that would remain permanently. So now Javier could stand and bear his full
weight, although it was still painful for him to do so.

"Are you okay?" she asked. "Do you need any
help?"

"No…thanks." His grimace morphed into a pain-streaked scowl, and his words came out in labored huffs. "I've…got it."

She hoped so. He'd just started to use those crutches, thanks to the seriousness of his fractures. He'd been through a lot physically, so there were going to be some tough days ahead. She wasn't sure if he carried any scars beyond what she could see, but she understood why his family had suggested that he get some counseling.

Since she'd already made a note of it in his chart, she wouldn't bring it up to him again.

"Does your family know you're moving to rehab today?" she asked.

"Yeah." He shifted his hips in bed, lifting the sheets and moving his legs to get into a better position. As he did so, he stopped and closed his eyes for a moment, clearly dealing with the effort and pain. "I told them about it yesterday, although I wasn't sure when the bed would open up."

She watched him move again, straightening his legs out a little more.

"Do you want me to call anyone and let them know which room you'll be going to?" she asked.

"No, that's not necessary. They're going to check with rehab before their next visit."

She waited a beat before adding, "I'm a little envious of you and your family. I know there's a downside to having so many people in your life, but there must be some wonderful perks, too."

"Yeah, there are." His expression softened, indicating that the pain he'd suffered from his trek to the bathroom had finally eased. "I take it you don't have many brothers or sisters."

"I just have one—a brother. But Justin and I aren't very close."

"Why is that?"

"I don't know." She moved toward the serape that was draped over the chair, then began to fold it so he could take it with him. "I suppose it's because he's nearly ten years older than I am. He also lives out of state, so we don't see each other very often."

"That's a pretty big age difference. Is he only a half brother?"

Leah could understand why he'd think so. Javier wasn't the first to make that assumption, especially since she and Justin didn't bear much resemblance to each other.

"Our parents got married young," she said. "They loved each other, but they separated and reconciled off and on for years. They finally got it together when he was nine, so they decided to have me."

"It sounds as though your childhood was probably a lot happier than your brother's must have been."

"In some ways it was. But when I was four, my mom was diagnosed with cancer."

"I'm sorry."

Leah didn't usually share that memory unless it was with a patient she wanted to help come to grips with his or her own tragedy, so she wasn't sure what to say.

It had been a long time ago, but she still remembered that sad and lonely period in her life, even though she'd tried hard to put it behind her.

"My mom lived another four years," she said, "although the last six months were especially rough."

"I lost my mother last year, and it was tough on all of us. I can't imagine how difficult it must have been for you as a child."

"It was a sad time, but things happen that are out of our control. And to be honest, it was almost a relief when she passed. She'd suffered a lot, especially at the end."

There'd been another good thing to come of it, she supposed. When her mom had been sick and in the hospital—the surgeries, the chemo, the radiation—Leah had grown close to some of the nursing staff, who'd offered a great deal of comfort and support to her mother, as well as to her. As a result, Leah had decided on a medical career while still a little girl. In fact, she'd never considered anything else.

"Were you close to your dad?" Javier asked.

One might think that would be the case, but that's not the way it had worked out.

"My father never was very good at dealing with his emotions—or with anyone else's. That's part of the reason he and my mom had those marital troubles in the early years. So he found it easier to go to work than to spend much time at home."

"He left you alone?"

"No, we had a housekeeper. But pouring himself into his business made it easier to deal with his loss and easier not to deal with mine."

Silence stretched between them as he pondered either her comment or his response. Then he said, "I've escaped into my work in the past. But I don't have kids."

Leah didn't need him to complete the chain of thought to realize they were on the same page. Being a father required a man to put his children ahead of himself. At least, that's the way it was supposed to happen.

"Don't get me wrong," Leah added. "My dad might not have been home much, but he loved my brother and me. He also provided all the nicer things in life. Justin and I were both able to attend a private college without having to work or get student loans. And I had a closet full of clothes and shelves loaded with toys and books."

Still, the "things" her dad had given her hadn't been able to make up for not having him around. Or for a house that was never really a home.

Even when Justin came back to Red Rock during his summer vacations, he didn't spend much time with Leah. He had a lot of friends he wanted to see while he was in town, so she was left on her own more often than not.

Of course, things really perked up whenever Aunt Connie came to visit. Her mom's sister came to Red Rock each Christmas and once during the summer. It was only natural that Leah had gravitated to the single woman who'd been a loving mother figure. Had Connie lived in Texas, rather than in Florida, things might have been different. *Better.*

Not that her childhood was all that bad.

Leah glanced at Javier, saw him watching her. A thought-provoking silence stretched between them as the seconds ticked by.

Goodness. What was she doing? Lollygagging and reminiscing while she was supposed to be working with other patients?

She glanced at the clock on the wall. How long had she been here? Just a couple of minutes, she supposed, but she couldn't stay. She had to get out of here before she said something she regretted.

Or before *he* did, because the intensity in his gaze was almost…unnerving.

Just the sight of him lying in bed, watching her like that, like he was going to slide over to make room for her to join him…

Oh, for the love of Pete. The man was recuperating from near-fatal injuries. He certainly wasn't having those kinds of thoughts.

So why in creation was she?

As she took a step back, preparing to return to work, Javier lobbed an easygoing grin her way. "You're spoiling me, Florence. I hope the nursing staff in the rehab unit is as good to me as you are."

Her heart warmed at the affectionate tease, yet her pulse rate slipped into overdrive, too. This particular patient was going to be her undoing, if she'd let him. But that was her secret.

So she returned his lighthearted smile, as well as his tease. "You're in luck. The rehab nurses are incredibly competent. The only one you need to watch out for is Brunhilda. They say she ran a torture chamber in a past life and isn't fond of men. So I hear tell she can be brutal at times."

"I'll keep that in mind." Javier zeroed in on Leah, saw the glimmer that lit her eyes, revealing a playful side he hadn't always been privy to.

He couldn't help but add, "Then maybe I ought to refuse to go and just stay here, where the nurses are fond of their male patients."

Her smile drifted away and she bit down on her bottom lip as if he'd struck a sensitive spot.

Was *she* fond of him?

Before she could respond, an orderly with a wheelchair entered the room, followed by a candy striper pushing a small cart.

For a moment, Javier wondered if Leah had been relieved by the interruption or sorry for it.

"Javier Mendoza?" the orderly asked.

"Yes, you've come to the right place," Leah said. Then she turned to Javier. "It looks like your ride is here. Do you have everything ready to go?"

"Pretty much." Javier threw off the covers, then made the effort to swing his legs over the edge of the mattress and sit up in bed.

He wasn't sure what was going on with Leah—or if they'd merely shared a few flirtatious but meaningless moments during his stay.

Either way, he'd always looked forward to her visits, even if it was to give him medication or run some test. And he hoped he'd see her again.

As he prepared to stand, he wondered what the old Javier would have said to her at a time like this. Without a doubt, that Javier would have jumped on the chance to ask her out, even at the risk of hearing her say no. But the new Javier wasn't sure which of his limitations were going to improve remarkably with rehab and which he'd be stuck with for life.

So he'd be damned if he'd pursue anything with her at this point. What man wanted his lover to double as his nurse or caregiver?

Not many.

And certainly not him.

He stole a glance at Leah, watched as she placed the folded serape in a white plastic bag that bore the blue hospital logo. She wore a quiet expression, a pensive one he'd give anything to read.

Did it bother her to see him leaving? Was she going to miss him?

Before Javier got a chance to either give it some serious thought or to shake it off completely, the orderly pushed the wheelchair closer. "Do you need my help?"

Javier would rather fall to the ground than to admit that he wasn't able to do something so simple on his own.

"No," he said, his movements slow and deliberate. "I can do it."

As he turned so he could lower his backside in the chair, Leah asked, "Are your things packed?"

"Not yet, but I don't have much to take. My shaving gear is in the bathroom, and I've got a few things in that closet."

"I'll get it for you." Leah headed to the bathroom, where she picked up his toiletries. Then she went to the closet and packed the extra pair of pajamas Rafe had brought, along with a pair of goofy-looking socks that served as slippers.

For a guy who'd always slept in the raw, the PJs were enough to make Javier feel as helpless as a child, which cast a dark shadow on his mood.

After Leah placed the bag on the cart, she gathered the rest of his things, including the flowers Savannah had brought him the other day. The other floral arrangements he'd received after his transfer from ICU to the third floor had died and been thrown out long ago, but the potted plants still thrived.

As Leah tiptoed to reach a philodendron from one of the shelves near the window, he watched her top pull up a tad. Too bad it wasn't short enough to show some skin....

Damn, it would have been nice to see her wearing that pair of tight jeans again, rather than those boxy scrubs. Still, she moved with a natural grace and style, no matter what she wore. In fact, there was something classy about Leah. And something sexy that the shapeless medical garment couldn't hide.

If the orderly and the candy striper hadn't been in the room, Javier might have uttered something flirty again. But it was best that he didn't.

Once the cart was loaded and he was seated in the wheelchair, he was tempted to ask Leah if she would come to visit him in rehab, but the question seemed a little too...needy. A little too weak. And for a guy who'd held the world by a string just two months ago, he wasn't about to do anything that made him feel any less of a man than he already did.

Besides, he had too much on his plate right now to be thinking about romance.

Yet he couldn't help wishing that she would come by to see him on her own.

Chapter Four

After the orderly wheeled Javier to the rehab unit, Leah remained standing in his empty room, taking a moment to feel the loss of the man who'd just left.

Talk about crazy. She rolled her eyes and started back to the nurses' station, only to find the doorway blocked by a petite brunette carrying what appeared to be a box of chocolates.

"Excuse me," the woman said. "I'm looking for Javier Mendoza. I could have sworn his brother told me he was in three-fourteen."

"Up until a few minutes ago, this was his room. You just missed him. He's been transferred to the rehab unit."

The attractive visitor knit her brow as though confused or disappointed.

"That's actually good news," Leah said, offering some reassurance. "After he spends a week in rehab, he'll be released from the hospital altogether."

The woman's striking blue eyes, which had been enhanced by a thick application of mascara, lit up. "*Oh*. Then that *is* good news."

Leah scanned the well-dressed visitor, who was in her mid to late twenties, wishing she could find fault with her appearance or her style, but she couldn't.

"Can you tell me how to find the rehab unit?" the brunette asked. "I've been waiting to visit until the family gave the okay."

"It's on the east side of the hospital. You'll need to go down to the second floor, which is the only access from here. Then follow the signs. You shouldn't have any trouble finding it."

Her perfect smile gleamed. "Thanks so much. You've been a great help."

"No problem." Leah returned the woman's smile, although her own fell short of sincere.

As she watched the brunette turn and walk away, her hips swaying, her high heels clicking upon the hospital floor, Leah realized she was the second beautiful woman who'd come to see Javier in the past three days. And since Rafe had obviously orchestrated both visits, it seemed like a natural jump to assume they were both old lovers—or maybe even current ones.

A green-eyed twinge, which felt a bit too much like jealousy, rose up inside of her, but she did her best to tamp it down. Why should she give a darn if women were clamoring for an opportunity to offer Javier some tender loving care?

The only explanation she could come up with was that some transference was taking place, the psychological phenomena that occurred when a medical professional found him- or herself attracted to a patient—or vice versa. They often imagined themselves in love when it was just a fleeting attachment taking place. And she wasn't going to fall into that trap.

So she shook off those lingering, inappropriate thoughts and feelings, as she headed back to the nurses' station, determined to focus on her work.

She'd barely taken a seat behind the desk when the phone rang. She answered it. "Third floor nurses' station."

"I'm sorry to bother you, but I just called Javier Mendoza in room three-fourteen, and he isn't answering. I spoke to his brother last night and he suggested I stop by to visit. But once I arrived in the lobby, I realized that I should have called first and made sure that it was…you know, okay with him. Is now a bad time?"

Probably, since the brunette who'd just come looking for him was probably arriving in Javier's new room about now. But Leah wasn't about to help the man juggle his lovers, so she said, "Mr. Mendoza has been moved to the rehab unit. It's on the east side of the hospital. Take the lobby elevator to the second floor, then follow the signs."

"Thank you *so* much."

Something told her that Javier wouldn't be anywhere near as thankful for her answer as the caller had been, but if he'd been dishonest in his relationships, then it served him right.

As Leah hung up the receiver, she couldn't help wishing that there really was a rehab nurse named Brunhilda—and that she'd been cracking her knuckles, waiting for Javier to arrive.

Oh, for Pete's sake. What kind of adolescent thought was that?

Still, in spite of a decision to put Javier Mendoza out of her mind for good, she couldn't help wondering how many women he'd been seeing.

More than he could keep track of, no doubt. Before the tornado struck Red Rock, he'd probably had a different woman on his arm every night of the week. And if that were the case, Leah was lucky he was gone. She'd never trusted cocky, overconfident men who refused to make a commitment or to keep their promises.

Just like Stephen Gardner, the man who'd broken Aunt Connie's heart.

When Leah was a teenager, Connie had spent a summer in San Antonio, where she'd met a handsome and charismatic attorney. She'd fallen hard and fast for him. And why wouldn't she? The man had wined and dined her until she was walking on clouds.

One night, she'd come home and told Leah how deliriously happy she was. "I'm calling a Realtor in the morning and putting my house on the market."

Leah had been thrilled, not only for Connie but for herself. She adored her aunt and hadn't been able to think of anything better than having her nearby so they could see each other daily. But before Connie could list her condo in Palm Beach or give notice at work, Stephen had ended things—over the telephone.

"I care for you," he'd told her, "but I think it's best if we take things slow."

Connie had been crushed, of course, but she'd decided to let him have a little space and time, hoping that he'd come to realize what she'd already known—that their relationship was meant to be.

Then, just days later, while Connie and Leah had gone out to dinner to celebrate Leah's birthday, they'd seen Stephen out on the town with another woman.

Connie was heartbroken, to say the least. And she'd immediately canceled her plans to move to Texas. When Leah had dropped her off at the airport, they'd both cried their eyes out—saddened by what would never be.

And even now, years later, Connie was different—more somber. The whole Stephen thing had changed her.

But enough of that. Leah wasn't going to stew over

the past, so she reached for the file of one of her patients. She wanted to double check the dosage of the new antibiotic Dr. Wang had ordered.

Before she could open it, Brenna, the LVN, approached the desk. "Have you got a minute? I'd like to ask you a question."

Leah looked up from her work. "Sure. What is it?"

"Do you know anything about Brice McNally, the new intern on the fourth floor?"

"No, not really. Just that he came here from Johns Hopkins and that he's supposed to be sharp. Why?"

Brenna bit down on her bottom lip, then shrugged. "I don't know. He…well, he asked me out. And I told him I'd think about it."

"Are you looking for advice?"

Brenna nodded. "Yes, I guess so."

"For what it's worth, I try to make it a practice not to date anyone I work with. It makes life easier that way."

"I had a feeling you'd say that." Brenna blew out a wobbly sigh. "And you're probably right. I need this job, and I don't want to have any problems at work."

Leah studied the young woman, saw the dilemma in her eyes.

"It's just that…" Brenna shrugged a single shoulder. "He's amazing, and I was so flattered when he asked me out. But I can see where things could get awkward. I'm not the only woman who's interested in him. Know what I mean?"

Leah nodded her agreement. Since she spent so much time at the hospital, both of her relationships had been with men she'd met on the job. And that's what had made things a little more complicated when they hadn't panned out.

"Sometimes those workplace romances can turn awkward," she said.

Brenna paused a beat, then asked, "Have you ever had one?"

"Yes, but it didn't last very long." About six months after Leah had landed the job at San Antonio General, she'd been attracted to one of the interns, too. They'd dated for a while, but the flirtatious doctor was too caught up in himself to settle down.

"If the opportunity came up again, would you reconsider?" Brenna asked.

"I actually did give it another try about a year ago, although that relationship bit the dust before it even had a chance to blossom." Several months after the breakup, Leah had agreed to go out to dinner with a radiologist she'd met in the hospital cafeteria. The guy was solid, dependable and family-minded, but he was also incredibly dull, and she hadn't been able to imagine living the rest of her life with him.

Sadly enough, she couldn't imagine living the rest of her life alone, either. But she'd come to think that having a husband and a baby might not be in her future. But that was okay. Her job and her patients had become her life's plan.

Brenna frowned, then shrugged again. "But what if I don't go out with Brice, and he turns out to be…"

"The *one?*" Leah asked.

Brenna nodded.

"That's the risk you'll have to take. I can only tell you what's right for me." And that's why she needed to steer clear of Javier—and not just because he was a patient. She had reason to believe that he wasn't the kind of guy to go the distance in a relationship. So Leah would be a fool to get involved with someone like him no matter how handsome he was, how charming his smile.

At the sound of rubber-soled footsteps, Leah looked to the left and spotted Karen, the RN who'd been assigned to Javier's room today, returning to the desk.

"I'm sorry for taking so long," Karen said. "First, I was at lunch, then I was called into an emergency situation in room three-twenty-one. What's going on?"

"Javier Mendoza has gone to rehab," Leah said, "so his bed is now empty. But other than that, things have been quiet."

"Good."

Karen was clearly glad to know that the floor hadn't been left shorthanded, while Leah couldn't help thinking it was "good" that Javier was gone.

Of course, she'd been left with a Texas-size hole in her day. And in spite of her resolve to steer clear of the man, the next morning, curiosity—or whatever else it might be—got the better of her and she decided to stop by the rehab unit during her lunch break to see how he was doing.

Javier, his head still damp with sweat, had stretched out on his bed after returning to his room following a difficult workout. He'd done all the therapist had asked and more, hoping to shorten his time in the rehab unit and return home. He'd be in therapy for quite some time, but at least he'd be out of the hospital.

Interestingly, his drive had returned, and he'd found himself pushing through the pain with a goal in mind. And *that* had felt good.

He glanced around his new room, which was smaller than the one he'd had on the third floor. That didn't matter, though. If all went according to plan, he'd be headed home in less than a week.

As his gaze landed on the clock on the wall, he realized that Leah would be taking her lunch break soon. If he was still on the third floor, she'd probably stop by to see him on her way to the cafeteria. She'd tell him that another nurse would be checking in on him while she was gone. But instead of slipping off, she'd hang around for a while, refilling his pitcher of water, making small talk.

He wondered if she was as dedicated to all her patients. Or if she'd found something special about him.

Damn. He was going to miss her.

But that wasn't going to get him anywhere. He had a goal in mind now, and that was to heal as quickly as possible and get back on his feet. Even if Leah felt the least bit interested in him, there wasn't anything appealing about a man who could barely walk on his own.

Still, in spite of his determination to heal and get back into the swing of his life, he couldn't help wondering what was going on back on the third floor. And wondering what Leah was up to.

He missed her smile, the lilt of her voice, the glimmer that lit those pretty hazel eyes—a shade that turned golden whenever she wore a green top.

The desire to see her again was hard to explain unless he admitted the obvious: he was missing Leah a hell of a lot more than he'd ever thought he would.

"Hey, there," a woman's voice sounded from the doorway. But it wasn't just any voice. It belonged to the nurse who'd captured his thoughts more often than not. And the dazzling smile she offered him was a far better gift than chocolate or flowers.

As she entered his room, Javier's mood lightened like a bouquet of helium balloons.

"Hey yourself," he said.

Leah made a quick scan of his new surroundings. "Well, what do you know? You're alone. I can't believe it."

"Yeah, well, it seems that they don't check on the

patients nearly as much in here as they did on the third floor. Or maybe the nurses aren't as competent."

"I wasn't talking about the medical staff," Leah said. "I expected you to have visitors. After all, I can't count how many women called or stopped by to see you, even after you were transferred." She wore a grin, but the way her eyes had flared, the tone of her voice...

Was she *jealous?*

Javier liked thinking that she might be, but he didn't want to play games about something like that.

"There couldn't have been more than three," he said, making light of the visits from Savannah and Maria, as well as the one from Jessica. "And they're just friends."

At least, they weren't any more than that now.

"As soon as I get my walking papers," he added, "the first thing I'm going to do is hunt down my brother and chew him out for sending every woman he meets to visit me."

The glimmer in Leah's eyes softened, as though she'd taken some comfort in his explanation.

"Nevertheless," she said, "I have a feeling things got a little awkward for you yesterday."

A smile stretched one corner of his lips. "Just a bit. But I've always found honesty to be the best policy. So there weren't any catfights, if that's what you're thinking."

She eased closer to the bed, but not quite close

enough. "I had a feeling you were a player in your pre-hospital days. So I'm sure you had no trouble soothing ruffled feathers—or rather, fur."

There it went again—that flicker in her eyes that seemed to chastise him for something she knew nothing about, something she thought he'd done, even though he hadn't.

"I dated two of those ladies," Javier admitted. "And while it might appear that they didn't know about each other, they did. I've always been up front and honest in my relationships."

"Which means what?" Leah asked, folding her arms in front of her as if protecting herself.

"I dated Savannah in the fall and Maria was a summer fling. But I never made either of them any promises."

"So you only date one woman at a time?"

"Usually. But if not, I've always told them that they weren't the only women in my life. If they weren't okay with that, then they'd find someone else."

"So you're a commitment-phobe."

"Not at all. I just haven't met anyone who made me want to settle down and have a serious relationship."

The truth of that statement struck something deep inside, something tender and raw. To be honest, and Javier wasn't ready to open up that much to anyone, he'd been reevaluating his life over the last few weeks.

He'd come pretty close to meeting his maker, and while he still had a long road ahead when it came to recovery, he'd taken a good hard look at his family. The fact that Rafe and Isabella had found love and were starting families reminded him of something he didn't have. Something he hadn't realized he wanted.

"So you'd settle down if you met the right woman?" Leah asked.

"Sure." But even if he actually found that particular lady, he couldn't very well settle down until he was back to his fighting weight.

That same dark shadow that had plagued him since coming out of the coma settled over him again, reminding him that life as he'd known it was over.

The two things he'd always counted on—his body and his brain—had failed him. And while he knew he'd see some improvement with time, he wasn't sure how much. That in itself was hard enough to deal with, but how was he supposed to get by without his mojo?

In the past, he'd been gifted with an inherent streak of luck, but it had run out on him the day that tornado struck Red Rock. And he feared he'd never get it back, that he'd never be back on top again.

"What's wrong?" Leah asked.

What was he supposed to tell her? That he missed the old Javier? That he might even be feeling sorry for himself?

Nope, he wasn't going to do that. So he conjured a phony smile and gave a half-assed shrug. "I guess the therapy took more out of me than I thought."

Then he risked a glance at her face to see if she'd bought his excuse, only to recognize sympathy as well as skepticism in her eyes. Great. Just what he needed. The only woman he'd found the least bit appealing in the past two months saw him as a wimp.

But maybe that was for the best. He wasn't anywhere near ready for a relationship—and who knew when or if that would change.

As Leah studied Javier at rest, his hair still damp from the physical workout he'd had earlier, her heart went out to him. She didn't doubt that he'd just gone through a grueling therapy session, but the pain he'd suffered and the effort he'd gone through hadn't put that shadow in his eyes. Something else was bothering him—that same something his family had noticed.

Unable to help herself, she eased closer to the bed and placed her hand over his. It was just a sympathetic touch, a gentle reminder that he had people who cared about him and a boatload of support. But when her fingers grazed his skin, a zap of heat shot clear to her bone and kicked her heart rate into overdrive.

As their eyes met and their gazes locked, something warm and charged with energy stirred between them. And for a moment, their brief connection melded into a solid and palpable bond.

Afraid to acknowledge whatever was simmering between them, she addressed his mood instead.

"What's really bothering you?" she asked.

He didn't respond right away. About the time that she was giving up hope that he would, he chuffed. "I'm not used to being laid up, crippled or weak, so I'm struggling with it, okay?"

His disclosure, his vulnerability, struck something deep inside her. The dedicated nurse within— or maybe it was the lonely woman—ran her fingers over his knuckles, along his wrist and settled on his muscular forearm. "There's nothing weak about you, Javier. You're recovering from life-threatening injuries that might have killed a man who wasn't in top physical condition. But you survived. And not only did you pull through, that strength and drive that made you successful before is going to make you better than ever."

With that, she removed her hand altogether, releasing the patient who'd stirred her in ways no one else ever had, and took a step back. She knew what to expect from the professional side of her, but those womanly thoughts and urges left her a little unbalanced and seeking a quick escape.

"Thanks for the vote of confidence," he said. "I've always been an optimist, but after the injury…"

Again, the nurse spoke up. "It's only natural that you'd focus on your limitations, but instead, look at how far you've come. Two months ago, your family called in a priest to give you last rites. And you've continued to improve to the point you can now walk. It's just a matter of time. You'll be home before you know it, and you'll hold the world by a string once again."

He didn't argue, but she wasn't sure that he was entirely convinced.

Still, that was reason enough for her to leave, to let him get back to the life he had once led. Because she didn't want to witness him morphing back into the successful real estate developer and entrepreneur who'd charmed attractive women right and left. Not that Leah had any real evidence that Javier was that kind of man—just a suspicion, a hunch.

Of course, even if he was a player at heart, maybe the accident had brought about a change in him, a good one.

Or was that merely wishful thinking on her part, brought about by transference?

She hoped that's all it was, since patients sometimes fell for their doctors—or their nurses, as the case may be—but that feeling was supposed to be fleeting. And the more time Leah spent with Javier Mendoza, the stronger her attraction grew.

"You're good at that," he said.

"At what?"

"Putting things in perspective, forcing me to see the whole picture."

Maybe so, but she wished she could actually take her own advice. She needed to take a big step back and let the rehab nurses do their jobs. Still, she thanked him for the compliment.

"So tell me," Javier said as the shadow in his eyes faded, leaving the whiskey-brown as clear and intoxicating as a double shot of Scotch. "How did you manage to get by this long without someone slipping a diamond on your finger?"

The crooked slant of his smile, the teasing tone of his voice, set off a buzz in her bloodstream and a sexual longing deep in her core. And by the intensity in his gaze, she suspected that she wasn't the only one feeling a rush of desire.

But she had to cut it off before it got out of hand, so she said, "I haven't met the right guy yet. And since I take my job seriously, I don't get many chances to meet eligible bachelors."

For a moment, she thought Javier would jump on the "eligible bachelor" line, but he didn't.

"You don't have to go out on the town to meet someone," he said. "There's got to be a doctor, lab technician or medical professional who's caught your attention."

Yes, once upon a time there had been. But neither of those relationships had worked out. And something told her that flirting with Javier Mendoza wouldn't work out so well either.

"I make it a point not to fish off the hospital pier," she said, even though her opportunity to "fish" anywhere else was limited due to her work schedule.

"That's too bad," he said.

Was it? The glimmer in his eye and his boyish grin

suggested that he might be imagining himself as one of those fish; she certainly was. But Javier Mendoza was off-limits to her—no matter where or how she'd met him.

"I'll settle down someday," she said. Then she added, "When the time is right."

And the timing couldn't be any worse than it was right now, even if transference or hormones argued otherwise. So she'd have to get her head out of the clouds, since a down-to-earth woman like her wasn't anywhere near ready to enter the high-speed dating world of an "eligible bachelor" like Javier Mendoza.

In fact, there were probably a lot of reasons she ought to refuse to go out with him. And as she began to ponder the first of them so she'd be ready with a quick response if he came out and asked her, she realized that she shouldn't have bothered.

In the end, no matter what she'd read in his body language or heard in the flirtatious tone of his voice, Javier let the subject drop, as if he'd never planned to ask her out or to see her again once he was discharged and went home.

Chapter Five

Five days had passed since Javier had entered the rehab unit and four since he'd last seen Leah. To say that he missed her visits was putting it lightly.

Their paths had crossed daily while he'd been on the third floor, yet with his move to the east side of the hospital, he might as well be on a deserted island.

He wasn't sure what that meant, but the truth was, as nice as the other nursing staff had been to him, he hadn't given anyone else a passing thought. The hospitalization and the long road back to recovery had taken an emotional toll on him, but Leah had managed to begin a healing process on the inside, on something he couldn't see.

So he would look her up as soon as he could walk

across the room without the use of crutches or a cane—a decision that gave him another reason to push harder during his physical therapy sessions.

Sure, she'd claimed that she didn't "fish off the hospital pier," but Javier wasn't a coworker. And he wouldn't be a patient at San Antonio General much longer if that bothered her.

So where was she now? Was she working today? Or was she trying to avoid him?

The thought that she might be distancing herself from him didn't sit well, even it if was probably for the best at this point in time. After all, he still grimaced in pain when he walked, still had to steady himself with a cane or crutches, still required time to recover from the effort to move from his bed to the bathroom, which he needed to do now. So there was no way that he'd ask her out until he was back on top of his game.

But when would he be fully mobile? What if by the time he did get back to fighting weight, she got involved with someone else?

And why did it seem to matter so much if she did?

Grumbling under his breath, he threw off the covers, rolled to the side and slowly swung his feet over the edge of the mattress. Then he reached for his cane and made his way to the bathroom.

Thanks to Isabella, who'd brought sweat pants and T-shirts for him to wear while in rehab, he no longer needed to wear those blasted PJs. So, in a sense, he'd taken one more step toward his goal of getting out of here and going home, where he could recover on his own.

After washing up at the sink, he splashed water on his face, then dried off with a towel before making the slow trek back to bed. Once he'd gotten settled on the mattress and the pain of walking had subsided, he tried to imagine himself at home, stretched out on the sofa, watching a ball game. But he'd been away so long. Two months seemed like an eon, and even now, when he was nearing the end of his hospitalization, the minutes ticked by at a snail's pace.

As he reached for the television remote, he heard footsteps moving down the hall and slowing at his doorway.

He wished he could say that a pair of Crocs had made the sound, but whoever it was wore a pair of street shoes. Still, he turned to the door just as his father entered the room carrying a familiar guitar case.

"What are you doing?" Javier asked, reaching for the remote to turn down the television volume. "Why'd you bring that here?"

"I thought you might like having it around." Luis carried the instrument to the window ledge and leaned it against the wall. Then he turned to Javier and smiled, looking for a moment like the man he'd once been before his wife's unexpected death had knocked him to his knees.

When Elena Mendoza died of pneumonia last year, the entire family had been heartbroken, but none as much as Luis. The couple had been exceptionally close and happy, so Luis now bore the ragged marks of grief that had deepened the fine lines on his face into wrinkles.

Not that he was bent or stooped, but his dark hair had also begun to gray at the sideburns and he no longer wore an easy smile.

At fifty-eight, he still had the physique of a younger man, but his shoulders didn't seem nearly as broad as they'd once been.

Had the fear of losing Javier so soon after his wife's death created additional stress on him?

Of course it had. And with that realization, a pang of guilt shot right through Javier, making him want to do whatever he could to ease his old man's worry.

"Thanks for thinking about me," Javier said.

"Yeah, well, music helps you relax. And you've been through a lot, first with your mom…and then the accident."

After his mother died, each of her sons had grieved in different ways. Javier had closed himself off to the world with only his guitar for company. And his music had helped a lot during those first few days after the funeral. But he'd soon found that focusing on his business deals had worked the best to ease the pain and to get him back into the swing of things.

Thankfully, his family had managed to rally, supporting each other, just as they'd done during Javier's recovery from near-fatal injuries.

"I would have brought your guitar to you sooner," Luis said, "but I didn't think they'd let you play when you were on the third floor."

"That's for sure. And the rehab nursing staff will have my hide if I create a racket."

Strumming the chords always took his mind off his troubles, but he wasn't about to play the thing while he was in the hospital. While tempted to ask his dad to bring the case closer, to open it up, he didn't.

"No one's going to complain if they hear you play, *mijo,* especially if the songs are soft and soothing. The other patients will probably enjoy hearing it."

Maybe so. He'd always found music to be therapeutic. Whenever business pressures built in the past, Javier would pick up his guitar and find a quiet place to play. Before long, a calming sense of peace would settle over him, leaving him relaxed and ready to face whatever challenges came his way.

Everyone who knew him—his family, teachers and friends—claimed he had the talent to pursue a career on the stage, but music was more of a hobby to him.

Instead, when given an opportunity to work with Roberto Mendoza, a distant cousin who had a thriving real estate business, Javier had jumped at the chance. And he'd never been sorry. His drive and ambition had served him well, leading to financial success and the purchase of quite a few properties he'd developed himself.

"Have you heard from Roberto?" Javier asked his dad. "I haven't seen him for a while."

"He's in Austin, putting together another real estate venture, but he'll be home soon."

"I'll bet he's missing Frannie and the kids."

"Without a doubt. He adores his family."

A couple of years back, Roberto had married Frannie Fortune, his old high school sweetheart. They were now raising their grandson Brandon, who was just a few months older than Maribel, their three-year-old daughter.

"I'm sure you're eager to get back to the office," Luis said, although an arched brow suggested he wasn't so sure about anything Javier was thinking or feeling. And he wasn't.

No one knew that he still struggled with being less than perfect, less than the best. As far as he'd been concerned, the guy who came in second was merely the first loser.

But Javier's father had suffered enough already, so he said, "You're right, Dad. I'm ready."

Maybe instead of strumming the guitar strings he ought to call someone and have them bring his laptop so he could access the internet, check a zillion emails and ease himself back to work.

Getting into the swing of things at the office might help him forget about Leah, too.

* * *

After Leah's last visit to the rehab unit, she'd forced herself to stay away from Javier for nearly a week, yet thoughts of him continued to plague her, especially when she knew he was only a five-minute walk down the hospital corridor. And as far as she knew, his time at San Antonio General was nearing an end.

What was she going to do when he was discharged and left the hospital for good?

She had no idea. Even with him being out of sight, he'd been on her mind more than ever. So in spite of her better judgment, she took some time during her lunch hour to visit him one last time.

With each stride she took toward the rehab unit, her steps grew peppier, her heart lighter—until she reached his room and found his door shut.

She would have turned away, but the guitar music coming from inside caught her by surprise.

Was he watching television?

There was only one way to find out, so she knocked lightly.

The strumming stopped, and the rich, baritone sound of Javier's voice said, "Come on in. It's open."

Leah reached for the knob, gave it a turn, then let herself inside his room. But the sight of Javier, sitting up in bed, with a guitar in his lap, stopped her in her tracks.

The past few days in rehab had given him a casual,

comfortable air. If he hadn't been in a hospital room, she might have forgotten that he was still a patient.

"Well, sing of the devil," he said, his deep and sensual voice wrapping her in a velvet embrace. "I thought you'd left me for good, Florence."

For the first time since he'd been transferred to her care, she was struck speechless from… What? Longing? Attraction? Desire?

His boyish grin and whiskey-colored gaze were almost mesmerizing, and it was easy to see how a woman could lose her head around him. In fact, Leah wondered just how many actually had.

She certainly struggled to stay in control.

In order to break the arousing eye contact and to end the awkward silence, she nodded toward the guitar he held. "I had no idea you were a musician."

"I'm not really. It's just a hobby."

The chords she'd heard hadn't sounded like those of a beginner or a hobbyist, but she let the comment go and made her way to his bedside, kicking herself as she did so.

Just as she'd feared, absence seemed to have made her heart grow fonder. And whatever she'd been fighting while in his presence had only grown stronger, more difficult to tamp down and keep under control.

"So how's it going?" she asked.

"It's all right. I guess I lucked out while being here."

"What do you mean?"

"I haven't seen hide nor tail of a nurse named Brunhilda. She must have quit right before they transferred me to rehab."

Again came that lazy grin, that teasing glimmer in his eyes.

Leah smiled, soothed by his easy manner while lured by the aura of sexual attraction that had built with each step he'd made toward full recovery.

What was she going to do about that? Hope that it ran its course before she fell in too deep?

Or maybe let it unfold naturally and see where it went?

"That *is* good news," she said. "So I take it the nurses have treated you well."

"Well, not as good as you did. But I don't have any complaints. I just wish that I could say the same thing about my physical therapist. He's an old military man, so he pushes hard. But he reminds me of my high school football coach, who used the same approach, which ought to be just as effective. With some hard work and perseverance, I'll be back up to speed in no time at all."

She certainly hoped so. He'd been through so much already.

As she scanned his room, which didn't have anywhere near as much medical equipment as his old one, she noticed quite a few get-well cards that had been prominently displayed along the window ledge.

"Isabella did that," he said. "And I didn't have the

heart to tell her I didn't want that stuff displayed for all the world to see."

The fact that he hadn't wanted to hurt his sister's feelings or to argue was a good sign.

"You didn't have that many cards before. Apparently, your many friends and admirers are coming out of the woodwork."

"Thanks to my brother. Rafe must have told everyone in town that I need cheering up."

Every *woman*, most likely.

Leah managed a smile. "It must be working. You're looking more upbeat."

"It's the music. It always does that to me." He strummed the guitar for a moment, again lulling her while luring her with slow but seductive chords. Then he looked up, smiled and nodded toward the door. "Would you mind closing that for me?"

"Not at all."

When she'd done as he asked and turned back toward him, he said, "Have a seat."

As she settled into the chair by his bed, he began to play a familiar tune, and she found herself drawn by both the man and his music. While he sang, telling the tale of a lady who was down on love and the cowboy who set out to mend her broken heart, the soul-stirring lyrics and music touched something deep within her.

When he finished, it took a moment to find her breath, let alone her voice.

"That was beautiful," she finally said. "I had no idea you were so talented. Have you ever sung professionally?"

"No."

"Have you ever considered it?"

"Not for longer than a moment or two. My family sometimes ropes me into singing for them at birthday parties and get-togethers, but not very often."

"I can see why they'd want you to sing."

He paused for a moment, then said, "Don't get me wrong. I don't mind doing it. But if performing was a job, it wouldn't be fun anymore."

Too bad, she thought. He had a wonderful voice—rich and seductive—as well as a great command of the guitar. It wouldn't take him long to build a fan base. But if getting on stage wasn't his thing, then he'd made the right decision.

She let the subject of his talent drop and said, "You're looking good. You even have a little color in your cheeks."

"My therapist and I worked outside for a while today. And I'm glad we did. Being in the sunshine and breathing in the fresh air felt great."

Maybe that's all he needed—to be out of the hospital and back on his feet. She'd have to mention that to his family if they brought up the idea of a counselor again.

Leah noticed an open laptop resting on Javier's tray table, which was a pretty good indication that he'd begun to move into the real world again. "I see you've been doing more than watching television these days."

He nodded. "I asked my dad to bring in a few things for me. I'm trying to play catch-up, but it's going to take a while. I must have a million emails to wade through, not to mention some online banking I needed to do. If I hadn't made two payments to the utility companies, I would've had turn-on fees—and no power or water when I got home."

She supposed his family had been too worried about him to think about making sure his bills had been paid while he was out of commission. From what she understood, his finances were solid, so he wasn't in debt, just behind on sending out checks.

"How much longer arc you going to be here?" she asked.

"A day or so maybe. Jeremy wanted to consult with my neurologist. He's going to let me know what's going on when he makes his rounds today."

"I'll bet your family is planning a huge celebration when you're discharged," she said, knowing how concerned they'd been, how supportive of him.

"I wouldn't be surprised, but I'm not up for any parties. I just want to go home and sleep in my own bed for a change."

She couldn't imagine being hospitalized for more than two months, but before she could comment, a knock sounded at the door.

"Come on in," Javier called out.

Jeremy Fortune entered. When he spotted Leah, he seemed a little surprised.

"I thought I'd stop by and visit Javier," she said. "I'd heard you were going to release him soon, and I wanted to say goodbye and wish him the best."

Jeremy nodded as if her explanation made total sense. But why wouldn't it? No one knew what she was thinking, what she was feeling.

Goodness, how could they when *she* didn't even have a clue?

"Looks like Leah stopped by just in the nick of time if she wants to say goodbye." Jeremy scanned Javier's room, then broke into a smile. "We're going to send you home, which we'd better do before you nest in here for good."

"I take it that I've been given the green light," Javier said.

"Yes, you have. We have another test we'd like to run before we cut you loose, but nothing major. I see no reason you can't go home this evening—unless you want to hold off until morning."

"No, I'd like to go as soon as I can. I'll call around and see if I can find a ride home."

"I'm off duty at six," Leah said before she could consider what she was offering.

"You wouldn't mind taking me home?" he asked.

She certainly ought to mind. What had she been thinking?

Visiting him at the hospital was one thing; she

could explain that to herself and whoever might ask. But if she knew where he lived, if she delivered him home, she'd be tempted to stop by to see him again. And then where would she be?

Of course, it was too late to backpedal now. "No, I don't mind at all. That is, unless you'd rather ask someone else to take you."

Javier tossed her a bright-eyed grin. "To be honest, I'd actually like going home with you."

Going home with her?

She knew what he meant. He was talking about the ride she'd offered. But she couldn't help thinking about getting him in her car, driving straight to her house, putting him in her bedroom and continuing to monitor his recovery and care.

But that was the most absurd and inappropriate musing she'd had in days. Still, she managed to conjure a carefree smile and said, "Great." Then she nodded toward the open doorway. "I'd better get back to work. I'll see you around six."

"Good deal."

Was it? She wasn't so sure. But as she slipped out his door and started down the corridor, she found herself wearing a silly grin and humming the tune Javier had just sung to her.

After Javier signed the discharge paperwork, he called his family to give them the good news: he was finally going home. Needless to say, they'd been over-joyed.

While he'd talked to Isabella she'd suggested that she and J.R. throw a party for him at their ranch, but Javier had asked her not to bother planning anything. He'd certainly regained some strength and built up a bit of endurance over the past week in rehab, but he had a long way to go until he felt the least bit normal.

As far as he was concerned, there was no real cause for celebration yet. He might be walking again, but he had a limp. And he still struggled to stay on top of the feeling that his once charmed life had been stolen from him.

His dad and his brothers, including Miguel, who'd flown in from New York City two days ago, and Marcos, who was spending all of his free time at home with Wendy and their newborn daughter, offered to pick him up at the hospital and take him anywhere he wanted to go. But Javier told them he already had a ride lined up.

He just hoped it hadn't been a mistake to accept Leah's offer. But she'd been the one person he'd looked forward to seeing, the only one who seemed to understand how he felt and what he'd been through, the one who had a ready smile and drew one from him without fail.

In fact, he'd been tempted to ask her out several times after he moved from ICU to the third floor—and again after he was sent to the rehab unit. But he hadn't broached the subject. After all, she deserved a man who had his life together, his future mapped out. And Javier wasn't there yet.

Since he'd packed his belongings a couple of minutes ago, including the guitar, he took a seat in the chair near the bed until Leah got off work and came for him.

Fortunately, he didn't have to wait very long.

"Hey there," Leah said as she walked into his room. "I just clocked out, so I'm free to leave. Is everything still a go? Are they still discharging you this evening?"

"Everything's done. All I have to do is ask for an orderly to wheel me out to the curb."

"Then I'll get my car and meet you there."

Five minutes later, Javier was carefully maneuvering himself from the wheelchair and into the passenger seat of Leah's black Honda Civic. "I appreciate your offer to take me home."

"No problem. Just tell me where we're going."

His first thought was to suggest they go out on the town, maybe have a drink at his favorite upscale country-and-western bar, but the old Javier was still out of commission. It would be a while before he stepped out on a dance floor again or heard another bartender announce last call.

"I probably ought to stop by the pharmacy," he said. "I've got a couple of prescriptions to pick up."

"Should we swing by the market, too? If you

haven't been home in months, you'll probably need to stock up on some food."

"Actually, I should be okay. I have a lady who comes in regularly—at least, she did before I was laid up. I called her yesterday and asked her to clean out the fridge, then to stock it for me." He'd also asked her to stop by tomorrow so he could pay her, and she'd insisted upon helping him to settle in.

"Sounds like you've got everything under control," Leah said as she gripped the wheel.

Not like before. But he nodded and said, "It's an old habit."

"You mentioned doing some online banking. I hope you paid your cable bill. You're going to need your TV."

He didn't know about that. He'd watched enough television over the past few weeks to last him a lifetime. And while it had helped the days to pass, he'd gotten pretty sick and tired of watching game shows and old movies, although he still enjoyed *Pawn Stars*.

Even ESPN, which had always been a favorite cable network, hadn't done much for him other than remind him of his physical shortcomings, so he'd steered clear of that channel.

So once he got home, he'd probably avoid TV for a while. He had a state-of-the-art entertainment center and looked forward to listening to some good music for a change.

"The utilities are working, and the house is in

order. So I've got everything under control." He stole a glance across the console, wondering if Leah was buying him being on top of it all.

Sure, his bills had been paid and Margarita had stocked his fridge and pantry with food. The TV worked and so did the surround sound system.

But the things he'd really enjoyed doing like morning runs, biking and playing tennis were lost to him. At least for the unforeseeable future. Still, he had Leah to himself for the next few miles. And he planned to enjoy every minute of their time together.

Chapter Six

After stopping by the pharmacy, Leah followed Javier's directions to his gated community and pulled up in front of the condominium he pointed out as his.

She had to admit that she was a bit surprised at the part of town in which he lived. Sure, she'd known that he'd been successful and financially secure, but she hadn't realized he lived in one of the more exclusive areas of Red Rock, which was impressive by anyone's standards. And she couldn't help commenting on what he'd probably heard a hundred times. "This is a great neighborhood."

"Thanks. It was one of the first developments my cousin Roberto and I worked on. I liked the location and the builder, and had been offered my choice of units. So I snatched this one because it's on the green-belt and close to the pool and the biking trails."

She couldn't help wondering if hc was going to invite her into his home, and not just because she was eager to see what it looked like on the inside.

"If you unlock the door," she said, "I'll bring in your things."

"I'll carry something."

"How are you going to do that? You're walking with a cane, remember?"

He grew silent. She hadn't meant to remind him of his limitations, but he was just getting to the point where he could walk from point A to point B. Why risk a fall now?

Minutes later, Javier opened up the door and turned on the lights.

"What a beautiful painting," Leah said as she spotted the brightly colored artwork he'd purchased in San Antonio.

"Thanks. Thc artist is especially talented. Isabella knows him and suggested I check out his work when I was decorating the place."

"It was a great suggestion," Leah said. "And you made a good choice."

After dropping off the first load of his things on the floor near the sofa, she returned to the car for the rest of them, the last of which were two potted plants he'd received during his stay on the third floor.

"Do you mind if I place these on the kitchen counter for now?" she asked.

"That's fine. Thanks."

While in the kitchen, she scanned the interior, taking note of the black granite counters and the stainless steel appliances that would be up to Emeril's standards. Then she returned to the living area, picking up on the scent of lemon oil and cleaning products, as well as noting the professional decor.

With its modern leather furniture and touches of chrome and glass, it could have been one of the models in the presale days.

In the living room, where Javier had settled on the sofa, she spotted a state-of-the-art entertainment center. And she couldn't help thinking the interior decorating had been customized with a bachelor in mind. Still, it required a comment of some kind.

"Your home is beautiful," she said. "And spotless. It hardly looks lived in."

"That's probably because it's been vacant for months."

That's not what she'd meant. But she let it go. He'd mentioned having a cleaning lady, so the woman had probably had plenty of time to spend polishing the place while he'd been gone.

"Have you had dinner?" she asked. "Do you want me to fix you something to eat?"

"That sounds good—if you'll join me. You've got to be hungry, too."

She was. And while the smartest thing to do would be to fix him a quick sandwich, throw back the covers on his bed, then skedaddle, she found herself saying, "Sure, why not?"

And that's the attitude she maintained for the next thirty minutes as she took a couple of chicken breasts from the freezer and defrosted them in the microwave. She found pasta and spices in the pantry, which she used to create a flavorsome dinner for two.

When she entered the living room to tell him dinner was ready and ask where he wanted them to eat, she found music playing on the stereo and the blinds opened to reveal a beautiful array of city lights.

Clearly, she'd been right about this being a bachelor pad. And about Javier knowing how to set the stage for romance.

Of course, with her wearing a pair of hospital scrubs, it was hard to imagine him having romance on his mind. And while that should be a relief, she couldn't quite muster a smile.

"Why don't we eat in here," Javier said, indicating the dining room table. "I haven't had a meal with any ambiance since… Well, since last year."

The tornado had occurred at the end of December, and while that had been a couple of months ago, technically he was right. But a second thought struck her.

He hadn't mentioned the tornado. Was that on purpose? Was he trying to put it out of his mind while he dealt with the aftereffects and his recovery?

Or was she reading way too much into it?

"I'll bring in our plates," she said, deciding to drop the subject completely. "What would you like to drink?"

"I'd like a glass of wine, but with the medication I'm on, I'll have to pass. But you can open a bottle for yourself."

She wouldn't do that. She still had a ten-minute drive home, and… Well, a glass of wine, added to a view of the city lights and a handsome dinner companion, made this meal seem way more than it was.

Again disappointment flared and raked over her like the needles on a cactus.

"I spotted some lemons in the kitchen. Why don't I make us some lemonade?"

"Sounds good to me."

Moments later, they sat down to eat at the formal dining room table, which provided an amazing view of the city. If she'd been dressed differently, if she'd worn some makeup or had done her hair, it might have felt like a date of sorts.

As it was, it was a quiet dinner for two between friends.

After they finished eating, she helped him settle in on the sofa. "I'll put the leftovers in the fridge. There should be enough for your lunch tomorrow."

"Thanks, Leah. I really appreciate this—the ride home, the meal, the pleasant company."

"You're welcome. It was nice, wasn't it?" She

nodded toward the kitchen. "I'm going to take the plates to the sink. I'll be back in a few minutes."

"Don't bother washing the dishes," he said. "The cleaning lady is coming by tomorrow to see if I need anything. So I'll have her take care of that."

Leah slowed her steps, then turned to face him. "I'm not leaving the mess for someone else to do."

"Margarita will be happy to have something to do once she gets here," Javier said.

Leah doubted that. She'd never had the luxury of having hired help. At least, not after growing up, moving out of her dad's house and getting a place of her own. But rather than make that comment, she said, "I'm not comfortable having someone else pick up after me."

"Believe it or not, neither am I. But you don't know Margarita. Trust me on this. She'll be delighted to have something to keep her busy."

Leah found that hard to believe. "Why do you say that?"

"It's who she is. When I was a teenager and our family lived in San Antonio, she was a neighbor. She didn't have kids of her own, so she kind of took to my brothers and me, making us cookies, taking us to the movies and that sort of thing. When her husband died, leaving her in a financial bind, she had trouble finding a job. By that time, my parents had already moved out to the ranch, where my dad works now, so I made a job for her, even though I'm not home very often. In fact, sometimes I leave a mess just so she has something to do when she arrives."

Leah tried to wrap her mind around what he was saying. He hired a woman for a job he didn't need, then went so far as to find things to keep her busy?

"She likes fussing over me," Javier added. "And it's kind of nice knowing that we're doing each other a favor. Besides, my mom asked me to look out for her, and since it was the last favor my mother ever asked of me, I plan to keep Margarita both busy and employed."

Leah waited for him to continue, but the conversation seemed to have stalled. And a whisper of sadness crossed his face.

Was he thinking about the promise he'd made to his mom? Or was he still struggling with her loss? How long had she been gone?

"When did your mother die?" she asked.

He paused for a moment, then said, "Two years ago this month."

His eyes glistened and he glanced out the window, as if searching for something in the city skyline. But she figured the only thing he was really looking for was an escape from his grief, from the memory.

"I'm sorry," she said.

"Yeah. Me, too. It was quite a blow."

Instead of remaining in the center of the room, Leah returned to the sofa and took a seat next to him—not too close, yet within an arm's distance.

"What happened?" she asked. "How did she die?"

"She had a chest cold and a cough. She expected it to run its course, but it only got worse. When we finally insisted that she see a doctor, she was running a high fever. We all figured a shot of penicillin or something like that would make all the difference, but it didn't. Apparently, her cold had developed into pneumonia—an exceptionally virulent strain that didn't respond to antibiotics.

"The doctor called an ambulance while she was still at his office. And they took her directly to the hospital. But by the time she got there, her fever had topped one hundred and five. And nothing brought it down. In spite of everything they did, she died that evening."

The story, the sadness, draped over Leah like an old cloak she'd worn once herself.

"We wish that we'd insisted she seek medical care sooner," Javier said. "But I guess that's water under the bridge now."

"Sometimes medical care isn't enough," Leah said, thinking about some of her patients who'd died in spite of medication, surgery or the latest treatments.

"My dad took it hard," Javier added. "I guess we all did. But he's kicking himself for not insisting that she see a doctor a few days earlier, when they might have been able to help her."

Was Javier feeling the same way his father did? Or

was he blaming someone—his father, the doctor or himself?

Leah reached over and placed her hand over his, giving it a gentle squeeze, trying to offer compassion, sympathy…friendship. "I didn't mean to dig up old memories."

"Don't worry about it. I've come to grips with her loss. But it's tough sometimes. We were actually pretty close, so I really miss her. And that's why Margarita thinks she has to look out for me. And why you need to leave some of the mess for her to take care of tomorrow."

Again Leah faced the possibility that she might have made false assumptions about Javier. She couldn't quite grasp how a man who juggled his romantic relationships would be the kind of man who'd call his mother his friend and grieve her loss two years later. A man who would create a job for a woman who'd made cookies for him as a child.

"So go ahead and put the leftovers in the fridge," he said, "but leave the dishes. Okay?"

"Can I at least let them soak in the sink?" she asked.

A smile spread across his face, chasing away the shadows of grief. "You drive a hard bargain, Florence."

Leah smiled, then reached across the seat and patted his hand one last time. "Why don't you stretch out and put your feet up for a while. I'll be back in a minute or two."

True to her word, she placed the leftover chicken and pasta in a plastic container before refrigerating it. Then she filled the sink with hot, soapy water and left the dishes to soak.

But there was no way she'd leave the kitchen without making sure she'd wiped down the countertops. What if she actually met Margarita some day? She wouldn't want the woman to think she was irresponsible or messy.

When she returned to the living room and spotted Javier lying on the sofa, she nodded toward the doorway that had to lead to his bedroom. "Do you want me to turn down the covers for you?"

"No, that's not necessary. I can handle it."

She supposed he could, so she said, "If there's nothing else I can do, then I'll head home."

"I don't need anything else—unless you'd like to hang out for a while. I like having you around."

She was tempted to stay and chat longer, but knew it wasn't a good idea.

"I've got a cat to check on," she said, even though Miss Kitty was probably fine.

Yet she still didn't move toward the door. Why was she dragging her feet?

She really ought to say her goodbyes and get out of here. But her reasons for dashing off no longer held any merit. After all, she hadn't known that Javier had such a tender heart. Nor had she realized there was much more to the man that just a handsome face, a sexy smile…and an incredible musical talent.

He'd loved his mother and had called her his friend. And he had a strong, loyal streak, not to mention a generous nature.

"Well," she said, "I should get out of here so you can get some rest. Do you have anyone who can stay with you tonight?"

"No, I don't need anyone here. I'll be fine."

Still she found herself hanging out, hanging on. And she wasn't sure why. At a loss as to what to say or where to go from here, she threw a question his way—one she couldn't help asking, "Would you like me to swing by tomorrow and check on you?"

Javier hadn't expected Leah to take such a personal interest in him, and he wondered what she would have suggested had he told her he didn't feel good about spending the night alone.

He wasn't the least bit uneasy about it, though. That's why they'd had him stay an extra week in rehab—to make sure that he'd do fine on his own.

So he said, "Sure. That would be nice if you stopped by tomorrow. But if something comes up, I understand."

"I've got a couple of days off and no real plans other than reorganizing my garage."

As Leah strode toward her purse, which she'd left

on his recliner, Javier got to his feet and reached for his cane.

"Where are you going?" she asked.

"To walk you out to your car."

"You don't need to do that."

"I know. But it's dark out there."

She smiled, revealing a pair of dimples he hadn't noticed while he'd been hospitalized. "That's what porch lights are for."

Still, as he got to his feet, she waited. Then she slowly made her way to the door, as if making sure she didn't get too far ahead of him.

At least that's what he told himself. Yet as he followed behind her, trying to catch a glimpse of her silhouette through those boxy scrubs and not lucking out, he couldn't help remembering she was a nurse. A woman who was only doing what came naturally to her—taking care of the sick and wounded.

Like it or not, he was one of her wounded, one of her patients. And while he liked the idea of her coming by again to check on him tomorrow, he realized she was doing it out of sympathy.

Sure, there *might* be something else going on, too. But nothing he wanted to cultivate just yet.

He probably ought to tell her not to bother going out of her way. He had more family and friends than he knew what to do with, and each one would be calling or stopping by to check on him.

But none of them was Leah. And she was the one he preferred having around.

He'd dated more than his share of women in the past—some just for dinner, others for more than that. Yet none of them had looked out for him the way Leah had. Or maybe he hadn't let anyone else see his vulnerable side or get this close to him before.

Who knew what was really going on, but he opted to go with the feeling, the desire to see her again.

When they reached his front door, she opened it. Then she flipped on the porch light. "See? I can make it on my own."

Yeah, and so could he—even if he wasn't at one hundred percent yet and had no idea if he ever would be again.

"I owe you," he said.

"No, you don't. I'm glad I could help."

They stood like that for a moment, his legs aching from the workout he'd had before leaving the hospital and threatening to give out on him. But he was willing to take the risk, just to stand upright—and next to Leah. To see her eye to eye, to see how her head matched up to his. How his lips would fit over hers.

"I'll see you tomorrow," she said, her voice soft, husky.

Her gaze locked on his and her spring floral scent swirled around overhead.

It took all his willpower to refrain from reaching

out and running the knuckles of his hand along her cheek, to seek the softness.

The struggle between lust and love was nearly killing him as he fought the urge to remove the clip from her hair, to free those silky auburn strands and watch them tumble down her back.

With the smallest effort, he could tip her chin up and press his lips against hers....

But he had a long way to go before he won the right to do that, and in spite of all the hormones and pheromone pumping between them, he kept his hands to himself and said, "Thanks for the ride and for fixing my dinner."

"It was my pleasure."

No, it had been *his*. And one of these days, if he pushed himself hard enough in physical therapy, he would do everything in his power to earn the right to pleasure them both—and in more ways than one.

As Leah turned and walked away, Javier leaned against the doorjamb, trying to support himself and to keep from collapsing.

Yet he was unwilling to turn around and close the door until she was gone.

All the way home from Javier's condo, Leah had gripped the steering wheel as though she could ensure staying in control of both her vehicle as well as life as she knew it.

Their evening together had been surreal, ending

with what seemed to be a romantic moment only to dissipate as quickly as it had risen. When Javier had walked her to his door to say goodbye, she could have sworn that he'd been sorely tempted to kiss her. Or maybe she'd just hoped that he would.

To be honest, she wasn't sure if she would have let him or not.

Okay, that in itself wasn't true. Last night, as they'd stood in the doorway, as his eyes had zeroed in on hers, she knew exactly what she would have done if he'd lowered his mouth to hers.

She would have kissed him.

But he hadn't kissed her. And to make matters worse, she'd asked herself why all the way home. Had she merely imagined their attraction? Was it only one-sided?

If that were the case, she'd really gone out on a limb when she told him she'd return the next day.

Once she'd gotten home last night, she'd gone through the motions of feeding Miss Kitty and giving her the meds the vet had prescribed for arthritis. Then she'd turned on the television, only to find her thoughts a million miles away.

Well, not quite that far. They were across town, with Javier.

She'd dreamt about him off and on that night and finally woke a little after seven with Miss Kitty snuggled at her feet and the morning sunlight filtering through her blinds.

If truth be told, she was sorry she'd volunteered to check on Javier. After all, it's not as though he was an only child and all alone in the world. He had a big support system, including a number of concerned family members lining up to visit him and to make sure he had everything he needed.

She'd met them all at least once while he'd been hospitalized and under her care, including the brother who lived in New York City.

Okay, so she'd committed herself to driving back to his house today for a visit. But that didn't mean she had to rush over first thing in the morning, which would make her appear much too eager to be a part of his life.

But isn't where all of this was heading? She blew out an exasperated sigh.

Too bad he hadn't mentioned anything about his feelings for her—whatever they might or might not be. It would have made it easier for her to deal with her own feelings.

She'd give anything to be able to compartmentalize her thoughts into a neat little box marked as inappropriate and out of reach.

After a light breakfast of fruit and yogurt, she threw a load of colored clothes into the washer, then went for a run.

When she returned, she took a shower and shampooed her hair, using the new products she'd purchased at the salon last week. She took care to choose a special outfit—something more feminine than the hospital scrubs she seemed to wear more often than not—and settled upon black slacks and a pale blue knit top.

Then she blow-dried her hair with a rounded brush, adding body and a little curl to the ends. When she was finished and pleased with the results, she applied a dab of mascara to lengthen her lashes, as well as a light shade of lipstick.

It was just after noon when she climbed into her car and drove to La Montana Vista, the complex where Javier lived. He'd given her the gate code last night, as well as the number of his unit, and she hadn't forgotten.

After parking at the curb, she made her way up the walk, then rang his bell.

She'd expected Javier to answer or to call for her to come inside, but a silver-haired woman in her late sixties swung open the door.

Leah might have worried that she'd transposed the house number had she not recognized the Spanish-tiled entry and the colorful Southwestern painting that hung on the wall.

"You must be Margarita," Leah said.

The woman nodded. "And you are...?"

"Leah Roberts. I was Javier's nurse."

The older woman brightened, then reached out her hand in greeting. "It's so nice to meet you, Leah.

Javier mentioned that you brought him home last night and prepared his dinner."

Leah's cheeks flushed warm. "I'm sorry for not cleaning up after myself."

"Oh, pshaw. Javier told me that he insisted you leave them. Please don't give it another thought. It only took me a moment or two to load the dishwasher."

"Well, good. I'm glad to hear it. And speaking of Javier, is he up to having company this afternoon?"

"I'm sure he would be, if he were here. But Rafe just picked him up and took him to his physical therapy appointment."

Since Leah hadn't mentioned what time she'd be stopping by or asked about Javier's appointment schedule, she couldn't blame anyone for missing him but herself.

"I probably should have called first," she told Margarita. "Would you let him know that I stopped by to see him?"

"Of course. He'll be sorry he missed you."

Was that true? Leah wasn't so sure. And the embarrassment, the uneasiness, only made her wish she'd kept her mouth shut last night, that she hadn't told him she'd stop by today.

As she turned away and headed to her car, the door shut behind her. Yet she still couldn't shake the lingering disappointment that she'd missed seeing Javier—or the stark realization that she might never see him again.

Chapter Seven

The wind was cool and breezy, the perfect March day for kite flying—if a guy was still into that sort of thing. But Javier had given up kid games and activities a long time ago.

It would have been a good afternoon for a run or a bike ride, too. Instead, he climbed behind the wheel of his Expedition and drove himself to rehab. Ever since his discharge from the hospital, he'd been relying on everyone else to do things for him, which had been a real pain. He'd always prided himself on being self-sufficient, in being one to offer aid to others.

So today he'd taken another step toward independence and control of his life again.

He'd had a standing twelve-thirty appointment

with his physical therapist all week, but he left his house early today, hoping to stop by the third floor to visit the nurses who'd been so good to him and drop off a box of chocolates.

Okay, so he was actually only looking forward to seeing one of them—Leah. And the candy was merely a ploy to make his visit look legit.

Margarita had told him that Leah had stopped by to see him that first morning after he'd gotten home from the hospital, but as far as he knew, she hadn't come back. He probably should have looked her up sooner, but he'd been determined to stand firm on his decision. He didn't want to strike up any kind of romantic relationship until he was back to normal—or at least until he was walking steadily without the use of a cane.

He was definitely improving and getting a little better, a little stronger, each day. But he still wasn't recovering as quickly as he wanted to. Yet after waking this morning, after spending another dream-filled night with Leah, he'd decided to talk to her again, whether he was limping or primed and ready to run a marathon.

So here he was parking in the visitor's lot, getting out of the car and reaching for his cane. He still had months to go before feeling even remotely like the man he'd once been, the man who'd been on top of his game, his career, his life. But Javier wasn't going to let another day go by without seeing Leah.

Moments later, after limping through the lobby and making his way to the elevator, he got out on the third floor and headed for the nurses' station.

Brenna, one of the LVNs who worked with Leah, was talking on the telephone and taking notes. When her call ended, she looked up at him and, as recognition dawned on her face, she broke into a welcoming smile. "What a nice surprise. You're *back*—and all in one piece."

"Well, not quite yet. But I am getting around on my own now, so I thought I'd stop by and say hello to the best nursing staff in all of San Antonio." He handed over the gold-foil covered box. "And to give you this as a token of my appreciation."

"Well, thank you," Brenna said. "Aren't you sweet?" Then she looked up at someone walking their way and called out, "Hey, Leah. Look who's here."

Javier expected the same reaction he'd gotten from Brenna, a bright-eyed smile that announced his visit had been a welcome surprise. But instead, Leah's lips parted and her eyes widened in a way that seemed...

Hell, he'd seen that expression once before. On the face of an old lover when they'd accidentally run into each other on the street. He'd always prided himself in being honest, in not dating a woman who cared more for him than he did for them, although that required a woman to be honest with him, too.

But he and Leah hadn't been lovers or even occasional dates.

Just what had been going on between them? And when had it ended?

"Hey," he said, for lack of a better opening. "I'm not faster than a speeding bullet or able to leap tall buildings at a single bound yet, but at least I'm mobile and driving again."

"I can see that." She finally smiled, but it didn't quite reach her eyes.

Was she sorry to see him?

Again he was struck with that old-lover feeling, the awkwardness. Too bad he didn't have any sexually explicit memories to go along with that I-didn't-mean-to-hurt-you feeling as well.

Leah had on a new pair of scrubs today—a pair of lime green pants and a matching floral print top. Her glossy auburn hair had been pulled back into a single braid that hung down her back. As usual, she wore very little makeup, although she was one of the few women who were beautiful without any of the usual enhancements.

Her natural beauty, those expressive hazel eyes, full lips…

Damn. When had she become so much more to him than a nurse? And why did he feel as though he'd somehow dropped the ball?

"It's good to see you up and around," Leah told him.

Was it?

"How are you doing?" she asked. "How's rehab?"

"It's tough, but going well."

She smiled, her eyes finally showing a sign of the warmth he'd missed seeing.

However, what he'd really like to see again was the expression her face when she'd left his house that night, when the pheromones had swarmed in the porch light. Maybe he should have kissed her when he'd had the chance, but he'd felt as weak as a newborn foal and had feared he'd fall on his face.

And no way did he want Leah to continue seeing him as weak and damaged.

But if he wanted to set things to right, to get back where they'd once been, he'd have to get her alone.

"When can you take a break?" he asked.

Again, her lips parted as if his question had surprised her even more than his arrival had. But she glanced at her wristwatch—one of those no-nonsense styles with a leather band. As she did, he found himself focusing on her delicate wrist, thinking that it ought to sport a diamond bracelet instead.

"Actually," she said, looking up, "I can probably take a break now. Let me check with Marie, who'll have to cover for me."

Javier gripped the counter of the nurses' desk and watched as Leah headed down the hall. Moments later, she returned.

"I've got about ten or fifteen minutes," she said. "Do you want me to find an empty conference room?"

"No," he said. "Let's go out to the rose garden instead. It's only an elevator ride and a short walk from here."

Her eyes finally sparked, as if his suggestion had been a good one, and she nodded.

Five minutes later, they'd left the hospital and began the trek outside to the rose garden, moving slowly thanks to Javier's limp and dependence on a cane.

"It's nice to see the buds opening up," Leah said. "It's usually a beautiful garden, but it's been pretty stark all winter long."

"Now that spring is here, it should be looking good again in another few weeks."

She nodded, scanning the quiet grounds. "When the flowers are in full bloom, it's a beautiful place to reflect or to steal a few quiet moments."

Javier wasn't so much interested in the colors or the beauty the rose garden provided as he was the privacy. He'd just wanted to get Leah alone, but now that he'd done that, he'd be damned if he knew what he would say to her.

His first thought was to ask her out, even though he was a far cry from being completely healed. And while the wisest thing for him to do would be to hold off a while longer, he'd missed seeing her over the past week and didn't want to lose out on what they had—whatever it was.

So he sat in one of the benches, with its green slatted seats and black wrought-iron frame.

Leah took a seat, too.

"I stopped by to thank you for everything you've done for me," he began. "Not just for doing your job, but for understanding where I was coming from, even when I wasn't sure myself."

"No problem. I'm glad I was able to help."

"I know, but it was more than help. You went above and beyond." He didn't dare tell her how he'd waited each day for her to show up in his room, how the hours lugged by whenever she wasn't working.

Leah glanced down at her feet and at the Crocs that matched her scrubs. He had no idea how many pairs she owned, but he suspected it was four or five—each one coordinating with several different professional outfits.

He imagined her wearing a pair of spiky heels and a slinky black dress, with her hair swept up in a stylish twist. What he wouldn't give to see her let loose a little, to be a woman for a change, instead of just a nurse.

They sat like that for a moment, with him tempted to say the words that revealed his thoughts and feelings rather than those that made more sense. Words that would be safer, wiser…

He couldn't go so far as to ask her out.

Or could he?

On numerous occasions, when their conversations had taken a personal turn, he'd noticed how she would smile one minute then turn shy the next. It was almost as if she'd been struggling with her feelings for him, as if torn between woman and nurse.

And wasn't that exactly how he was feeling? Torn between being a man and a patient?

So now what? He had her alone for a few minutes longer. Where did they go from here?

"What did you want to talk to me about?" she asked.

"Mostly, I wanted to thank you for driving me home last week, for fixing my dinner. And also for stopping by to see me again the next day. I'm sorry I missed you. I tried to call but your number is unlisted. I'd kind of hoped you'd come back or leave a number where I could get a hold of you, but you didn't."

There. How was that for letting her know that he'd wanted to see her again without committing to anything else? Was it enough? He certainly hoped so.

The late morning breeze kicked up a bit, blowing a loose strand of hair across her cheek. As she swiped it away, she said, "I just stopped by your house because I'd told you I would. But I didn't see any reason to go back. You were in good hands. Margarita seemed both caring and competent. And your family was obviously taking you to your appointments."

Did she think he no longer had need of her? When it came to being his nurse, that might be true. But when push came to shove, he'd quit thinking about her as his personal Florence Nightingale a week ago—maybe even longer.

He turned to the right, his knee brushing against hers and jolting them both with a surge of physical awareness.

Yes, they'd both been jolted, because she'd been studying those ugly green shoes of hers, then the moment their legs had touched, she'd shot a glance his way and zeroed in on him.

As their gazes met and locked, that same swirl of pheromones kicked up again, urging him to reach out to her, to draw her close, to kiss her or to make some kind of romantic move.

But then what?

He couldn't afford to be that bold right now, especially when he had no idea if and when he would fully recover. Yet in spite of his best intentions and his conflicting thoughts, he couldn't help seeking out some middle ground.

"I'd like to take you out to dinner some night," he said.

"You don't need to do that." She brushed aside that same pesky strand of hair from her cheek again. "I was just doing my job."

They both knew she'd gone the extra mile time and again. And that the seeds of something sexual or romantic hovered over them—both then and now. And while he had no doubts about his ability to make love with her—and to make it good for both of them—he couldn't offer her much more than great sex and a less than perfect body.

Still, he pressed on, wanting her to know the direction his thoughts were heading.

"I'm not asking you to dinner as a token of my appreciation," he said. "I just thought it might be nice to see you wearing something other than scrubs. To sit across a candlelit table. Maybe to toast the future—whatever it might bring."

There. He'd done it. Laid his cards on the table, just to see what she'd say. And if she threw it right back in his face, he wasn't sure what he'd do. He'd never had to deal with something like that before.

"You want to date me?" she asked, lips parting again, her eyes growing wide.

Her expression—disbelief or whatever it was—set his heart on end, and he figured he'd better backpedal. It was one thing knowing that he wasn't good enough for her yet and another to know she was thinking the very same thing.

Still, it's not as though his ego couldn't handle rejection. So he said, "Yes, I suppose you could call it a date."

When she didn't immediately respond, he added, "Not right away, of course. I've got a lot of work to do in rehab yet."

Damn. Why had he admitted that he wanted to go out with her before he was ready to? He hated laying his vulnerability on the line like that.

But he didn't want to lose his opportunity to be with her either. And that was just plumb crazy since he'd never lacked having a romantic interest in his life. And he'd have someone again—as soon as he was walking without that damned cane.

Yet no other woman interested him right now.

"I don't know what to say," Leah said. "I've never dated a patient before."

"Yeah, well, I've never dated a nurse before either. But for the record, I'm not your patient anymore."

So why wasn't she jumping at the chance to go out with him? Her hesitancy was a first for him.

Of course, that's probably because he only asked women out who appeared to be interested in him.

And while he'd sensed there was something brewing between him and Leah, he might have been wrong. Damn. Had he lost his touch with women, with his ability to sense their romantic interest?

He wasn't sure. But he wasn't going to grovel or spin his wheels any longer, so he reached for his cane and, using the bench's armrest to steady himself, got to his feet.

"Give it some thought, Florence. But there isn't any rush. By the time I'm actually ready to take a woman out to dinner again, you'll probably be married with a couple of kids."

She merely sat there, her eyes still wide, her lips parted.

Okay, so he'd definitely lost his touch completely. He could have sworn Leah was feeling something for him, even though they'd never talked about it.

A slow smile slid across her face. "I doubt that I'll be married for a long, long time. My job is my life."

She hadn't said yes or no to his question, and he couldn't help wishing he'd held his tongue, that he'd kept his thoughts to himself.

After all, why would someone as perfect as Leah want to get involved with someone who was only a shadow of the man he'd once been?

Rather than let her sense his vulnerability, he slapped on a happy-go-lucky grin and shrugged it off. "Relax, Florence. It was just a wild-ass idea. Maybe I'll stop by the hospital to see you in a couple of months. We can play things by ear."

Then he forced a chuckle, as if he'd been joking all along, and glanced at his wristwatch. "We'll, I'd better go. I've got a rehab appointment in a couple of minutes, and I'm not as quick on my feet as I used to be. Thanks again for being such a top-notch nurse. You deserve one heck of a raise."

Then he turned and walked away, pushing himself to increase his pace, just so he didn't have to risk another conversation with her.

Or to give her the idea that her reluctance to respond had been a lot more painful than telling him the truth—that she didn't want to go out with him.

As Javier limped away, Leah sat dumbstruck on the bench. She hadn't known what to expect when he'd asked to talk to her in private. Or why he'd suggested they walk out to the hospital rose garden, the one place that she chose when she needed to commune with God or nature, the one place she allowed herself to reminisce about the past and to dream about the future.

She'd thought he might have a medical question for her, something he hadn't wanted to discuss with anyone else. But he'd just asked her out on a date.

At least, she'd thought that's what he'd done. He'd also implied that he wanted to have dinner with her several months down the road.

Why was that?

And why not now?

Sure, the question had taken her aback. He'd asked her in such a roundabout way that she hadn't known what to say, how to respond. And when she'd been tempted to agree—whether that was wise on her part or not—he'd treated the whole thing like a joke.

At that point, he'd dropped the subject as though he'd reached out and grabbed the heated end of a curling iron.

Or course, even if he'd asked her out with a bottle of chilled champagne sitting in an ice bucket, along with two crystal flutes and a bouquet of roses, she would have been even more surprised, more speechless.

And she wasn't entirely sure what why was. While he'd been in the hospital and under her care, he'd flirted with her at times, but he'd never gone further than that.

And he hadn't actually done so now.

Either way, he'd just walked off, leaving her to solve the puzzle on her own.

Or had her hesitancy caused him to retract his question altogether?

Something told her he'd gotten the wrong message from her. Or maybe she'd been the one to confuse the issue.

For a woman who'd sat on this very bench on more than one occasion, wondering if she'd ever meet a special man, she'd certainly botched things up with Javier.

Not that he was the kind of man she ought to date. But he was definitely appealing in more ways than one.

She couldn't let him go without explaining herself and her hesitation. So she got to her feet and started toward him. "Javier? Wait up."

He stopped and turned. "What is it?"

She nearly froze for a moment, then pressed on.

"I'm sorry for not speaking up sooner. I guess the whole idea was a little surprising. But I'd like to go out to dinner with you. That is, if you're serious about it."

He studied her for a moment, as if she might be lying, as if she might be stringing him along. "It was just a thought I'd had."

And one she found irresistible.

"I probably should have called ahead and let you know I was going to stop by," he added. "My visit had to throw you off stride, especially since we haven't seen each other in a week or so."

"I was surprised to see you," she admitted.

"I'm not sure why you didn't come back to my house—unless you're trying to avoid me. And if you'd rather we not see each other again, that's fine, too. Just say the word."

"I made it a point to stay away, but not because I'd been trying to avoid you."

Okay, so that wasn't entirely true. She'd been trying to *forget* him, although it hadn't worked. No matter how many books she picked up or how many TV movies she'd tried to watch, Javier had remained on her mind.

"You don't have to explain, Florence. No harm, no foul."

"I think you're missing the point."

He stood there, as if daring her to explain. So she finally admitted what she'd been fighting for weeks on end.

"I care about you, Javier. Probably more than I should. And I'm not sure it would be in either of our best interests if we dated."

His eye twitched ever so slightly.

"You lead an active social life, and I'm pretty much a work and homebody."

"Yeah, well, my life has been curtailed as of late, and I'm not sure if that's going to ever change."

"Of course it will. You'll be back to your old self in no time at all."

He nodded as if he agreed. But something in his eye, in the way he tensed his lips, said, *Yeah, right.*

"For whatever it's worth," she added, "I'd like to go to dinner with you whenever you're up for it. And I doubt I'll be married by then."

As much as she worried that they were both making a big mistake, that he would be better off with a classier woman, that he ran in a different social circle than she did, she reached into her pocket and pulled out a small notepad and pen she kept handy.

"I'll give you my number, and you can do whatever you want with it." She looked up, caught his eye, then gave him a little wink. "Well, other than give it to someone else."

"You don't have to do that," he said.

What? Give him her number?

Even with the many doubts she had, she still had to admit that she felt something for him. And that it might be a bigger mistake not to give it to him.

What if she *could* trust her feelings? What if the two of them were better suited than she thought?

No closer to an answer, she scratched out her telephone number on a blank sheet, then tore it from the pad and handed it to him.

Javier took the paper from Leah, glad to have a

way of contacting her outside the hospital, yet realizing she hadn't given it freely to him.

"I'm not looking for your pity," he said.

"Pity is the last thing I feel for you."

He searched her gaze, her expression, looking for a sign of truth. "So you admit to feeling something?"

"Yes, but I'm not sure what it is. There's some definite attraction, but I'm afraid it might only be a case of transference on one or both of our parts."

"What's that?"

"It's a psychological phenomenon that occurs when a medical professional finds himself or herself attracted to a patient and vice versa. And it's way more common than you might think… Some patients actually think that they're falling for their doctors or nurses but the feeling isn't lasting. And it's not real." She took a moment to catch her breath, then continued, the words flowing from her mouth in a nervous rush. "It's not ethical for medical professionals to get involved with their patients, so I thought it was best to let those feelings run their course. And so I stayed away for a week…. But it's still a struggle. And I'm not sure why that is."

Javier took a step closer, reached out with his free hand and gripped her shoulder. "You're rambling, Florence. And I've never seen you like this. What's going on?"

She took a deep breath, then slowly blew it out as though she could banish her nervousness and reel in her jabbering. "Being around you is making me this way. I'm attracted to you. And I'm struggling with it, okay? I want to do the right thing, and I'm not sure what that is. And so I'm…"

Javier had no idea what had set her off like that. But the one thing he did gather was that she was attracted to him and fighting it for some reason. Although she was blaming it on transference or some crazy thing, rather than taking it for what it was.

She was flat-out flustered by their conversation— and so damn cute—that he couldn't help but grin.

Nor could he keep from removing his hand from her shoulder, cupping her jaw and drawing her mouth to his.

Chapter Eight

Leah's heart skipped a beat the moment Javier touched her shoulder, let alone her cheek. And she nearly flatlined as their lips met, as their breaths mingled. She reached out for his waist to steady herself, even though he was the one who held a cane.

The kiss, which had started out both sweet and sensual, deepened, their mouths opening just as though they'd been lovers for years. Just as though the dreams she'd been having about him every night for the past two weeks had decided to come true right this moment.

Still, she continued to kiss him—to brush her tongue against his, to dip, to taste. For a moment, she forgot who she was, let alone where she was—

outside the hospital, where any one of her colleagues might glance out a window and see her. But having witnesses didn't seem to matter one little bit right now. Not while she was making note of the fact that Javier Mendoza was the most talented kisser she'd ever known.

Not that she was an expert in the art of foreplay by any means, but just the same, she knew what she liked and how it affected her. And this one?

Oh, wow. What a kiss. Talk about fireworks—and it wasn't anywhere near July.

She leaned into him, knowing better yet yearning for more of the wet and wild heated assault of her mouth.

As he slipped his arms around her, drawing her close, his cane slammed onto the ground, bringing her to her senses.

Bringing them both to their senses.

She slowly pulled her mouth from his, placing her hands on his chest and gripping his shirt as if she could push him away and hold him close at the same time.

What was she doing?

Her cheeks flushed warm with embarrassment— or maybe as a result of raw desire. She had no idea what it was, but she had to gain control of herself. Goodness gracious. She'd have to go back to work in a matter of minutes.

Ignoring the awkward now-what discussion that

was bound to come up, she bent to pick up his cane. After all, what if he fell? What if he hurt himself all over again?

She tried to brace herself and Javier at the same time as she dropped down in front of him, past his belt, over his…

Of for Pete's sake. As she made eye contact with his fly, as she grew aware of a stirring erection, she swallowed—hard. Her heart began to pound like a jackhammer and she didn't know what to do, what to say.

For the second time in minutes the man had left her speechless and nearly brain-dead.

She reached for his cane, then rose to her feet and handed it to him, this time focusing on anything but the man in front of her. Yet her head was still spinning.

"Well, I guess that answers one question," he said.

She had no idea what he was talking about because, when it came to questions, she had a ton of them herself and didn't know where to begin.

"What's that?" she asked, finally making eye contact and hoping her cheeks weren't flushed as deeply as she suspected they were.

"You were right, Florence. You are feeling more than pity for me."

"I don't know what I'm feeling, remember?" She took a step back and crossed her arms.

"Well, there's definitely some chemistry brewing between us."

She couldn't argue that point.

"Maybe we should try kissing again, just to make sure it was the real thing."

Her cheeks heated even more, setting off a rosy flush. no doubt. But it had all been real—the kiss, the arousal, the desire for more. Yet now it was her turn to shrug off the feelings, the magic.

"We'll see about that. But not here."

He scanned the rose garden. "What's wrong with this place?"

"Nothing. It's actually a special place." And now, each time she came back out here, she would think of him and the best kiss she'd ever had.

He cocked his head slightly. "Do you come out here very often?"

She nodded. "Sometimes during my breaks I'll come out here to read, to eat lunch and to reflect." She turned and scanned the bushes that were just starting to bud and show a bit of color. "A few months ago, I had a patient who reminded me of my mother. She had cancer, too. And after we had to tell her that the treatments weren't working, that she was going to die in a matter of weeks, I came out here to keep from bawling my eyes out in front of her."

"Did it help?"

She nodded. "Yes, some."

"So it's a sacred place."

"No, it's not that. I've had a lot of quiet times out here, lost in my thoughts and dreams." And now those dreams were going to include Javier, whether she wanted them to or not.

And even if she never saw him again, every time she walked out to the rose garden, she'd relive that kiss again in her memory.

"I'm not the only one who takes refuge out here," she said, hoping to steer the conversation away from what the rose garden was going to mean to her from here on out. "And it can be seen from the windows of half the rooms in the hospital."

"So you're concerned that someone may have seen us?"

She didn't know what concerned her the most. She just needed to get her thoughts back on track. So she glanced at her wristwatch, noting the time. "We're going to have to talk about all of this later. I have to go back to work now."

"I don't suppose you'd like a kiss goodbye." He cracked a boyish grin.

"To be honest?" A smile crept across her face, matching the one on his. "I'd like that—a lot. But that's not going to happen. I'm going to have a hard time keeping my mind on my patients as it is. And that's not good."

"Okay, I'll tell you what. Go on back to work and do your best to put it out of your mind. We can talk about it tonight over dinner at my place. Nothing fancy."

She didn't know what to say, which was bothersome in itself. She'd never felt so indecisive in her life.

"I'll see you around seven," he added, clearly assuming that she would say yes.

And maybe he knew her better than she thought, because she found herself nodding in agreement as she turned around and walked back to the hospital.

Javier had never planned to kiss Leah—at least, not yet. He'd wanted to wait until she met the man he once was. And while kissing her had complicated things, it had also convinced him that he needed to resort to Plan B, an option he hadn't come up with before.

As much as he'd wanted to be one hundred percent when he asked her out, he couldn't put that off any longer. No way did he want to risk her hooking up with someone else in the meantime. And the kiss— as mind-blowing as it had been—had convinced him to alter his plans.

So he'd asked her to come to his house for dinner tonight, hoping to buy some time to figure out what he wanted to do about her. And kissing her again was definitely on the top of his list.

Damn. He'd known it would be good between them, he just hadn't realized how good. They'd definitely be sexually compatible if things progressed that far. And right now, he couldn't see any reason they wouldn't—as long as he kept improving.

So after she'd gone back to work, he'd made the trek from the rose garden to the rehab unit, where he'd had one heck of a workout session, pushing himself hard, wanting to get better as fast as he could.

And then he'd gone home and crashed for a while.

He hadn't given dinner much thought when he'd invited her. If he'd been steadier on his feet, he might have thought about grilling something.

Too bad Margarita had taken the afternoon off to visit her sister, who was visiting from Guadalajara. He would have asked her to whip up one of her specialties before going home and leaving him and Leah alone.

As it was, he decided to drive to Red and order takeout. After getting out of his car, he limped to the entry of the family-owned restaurant his brother Marcos managed. He'd barely reached the hostess desk when Marcos spotted him and broke out in a smile.

"It's good to see you up and around, Javier. We're going to have to schedule a golf match soon."

"I don't know about that. The only thing I've been able to swing these days is my cane."

"That may be the case, but it's great to see you standing upright. You're looking good." Marcos reached for a menu. "Are you meeting anyone? Or is it just you?"

"Actually, I just want to order some takeout."

"We can do that. What'll you have?"

As Marcos handed over the menu, he said, "By the way, Wendy and I are having a little party next Friday night. Now that Mary Anne is home, we're inviting everyone to stop by for an open house. I hope you can make it."

"I wouldn't miss it for the world. Would you mind if I brought a friend?"

"Not at all. Who is she?"

"What makes you think I'm bringing a woman?"

"Because you'd never bring one of your golf buddies or your business partners to a family gathering. In fact, you'd never bring a regular date, either. This woman must be special. Who is she?"

Javier wasn't sure how to address the idea that Leah was special, even though she was. He wasn't sure if he wanted to let his family know that he'd found someone worth dating for a while exclusively.

"It's Leah Roberts, my nurse."

Marcos grinned. "I had a feeling something was going on between you two, but I kept quiet so I didn't jinx it. Now that I'm happily married, I'd like to see all my brothers find what I've found with Wendy."

"I don't know if things are going in that direction," Javier admitted. "We're really just…tiptoeing around the idea of a relationship. But she knows most of you anyway. And—"

Marcos gave Javier a little jab. "Don't stumble over

an explanation on my account. We'd love to see Leah, so feel free to bring her along. I won't mention anything to anyone about you guys dating, although I'm not the only one who noticed the way you looked at each other."

Javier ought to object, but the truth was, he'd looked at Leah differently than he had the other nurses. And she'd been looking at him in the same way.

He had no idea what would become of them as a couple, he just knew that being with her felt right.

Leah couldn't explain why she'd agreed to have dinner with Javier, since she had good reason not to get any further involved with him than she was. But the simple fact of the matter was their kiss had changed things.

So after getting off work, she quickly stopped by her house to change into street clothes.

If she'd listened to her head instead of her hormones, she wouldn't have gone to the trouble. As it was, after she'd freshened up, she chose a pair of low-waisted khaki slacks and a green top, as well as a lightweight sweater. Then she drove to his house, arriving a minute or two before seven.

Javier must have been watching for her because he opened the door before she had a chance to ring the bell.

He cast an appreciative gaze over her, then smiled. "You look great, Leah."

"Thanks." As much as she'd wanted to claim that kiss hadn't affected her as deeply as it had, that she was immune to his charm and that dazzling smile, she warmed at his praise, which she'd secretly been seeking all along.

"Come on in," he said, stepping aside for her, then closing the door once she'd gotten inside.

"You must be hungry." He led her to the dining room table, with the large bay window providing a romantic view of the city lights. "And since I picked up food for us, it's probably best if we eat first. We can talk over dinner."

Minutes later, they sat across the candlelit table with a Mexican feast spread before them. Javier had chosen grilled chicken, lightly seasoned, along with Spanish rice and a salad with what appeared to be a light sprinkle of cotija cheese over an avocado-cilantro dressing.

"This looks delicious," she said.

"I hope you like it."

"I'm sure I will."

After they'd both picked up forks, he said, "I want you to know that I didn't plan on kissing you in the rose garden today."

She certainly hadn't planned it, either. Nor had she expected him to launch right into the subject before she'd gotten a bite into her mouth. But that's why he'd invited her and why she'd agreed to come.

"I'm not in a position to jump into a romantic relationship with anyone right now," he added. "I've got to focus on my rehab."

That was good, wasn't it? She ought to be pleased to hear it, but an unwelcome stab of disappointment struck hard.

Was he giving her a breakup line before they'd even discussed dating?

"But when I'm ready for one," he added, "I'd like it to be with you."

Leah's heart leapt as a thrill shot through her. Was he indicating that if and when the time came he'd choose her exclusively? That the women who'd come by to visit him in the hospital, called on the phone and sent all those get-well cards would be history? That his days of playing the field would be over?

Aunt Connie had bought that line once, when she'd believed a happy bachelor had found her special and unlike the other women he'd been dating. And that false belief had only led to heartbreak.

Or was Leah reading too much into his simple comment? He'd only mentioned that he wanted to have a relationship in the future. Not now.

"You're not saying anything," he said.

Goodness. She'd been fighting her feelings for him for so long, convincing herself that her emotions couldn't be trusted, that she didn't know quite how to respond.

What if transference had nothing to do with any of this? What if her feelings for him were real?

"I'm…" She set her fork down on her plate. "I'm not sure what to say, Javier."

"There's something going on between us," he said. "Something too big to ignore. I've known it for some time, and I think you have, too. That kiss we shared this afternoon, along with your response to it, are proof enough for me that whatever we're feeling is mutual."

He had a point. The physical attraction—at least on her part—was nearly blinding with intensity. But was it also blinding her from reality? Was she seeing Javier clearly? Could she trust him when he said he was feeling it, too?

"That kiss was amazing," she finally said. "I'll grant you that. And I'm attracted to you. But you're right. Jumping into something at this point in time isn't going to do either of us any good."

"Then we're in agreement there."

Were they?

Then why was she tempted to ask when she'd see him again, when they'd have another opportunity to kiss?

And why did she fear that he only wanted a friendship or a relationship with her to help see him through rehab, when he'd be back to the old Javier?

And who was the old Javier? Her instincts told her he was a lot like the man Aunt Connie had fallen for, a lot like the intern Leah had once dated—a dyed-in-the-wool bachelor who moved from one woman to the next with the ease of changing his socks.

A man she'd be wise to avoid.

Instead, she opted to change the subject. "This chicken is out of this world. You'll have to give my compliments to the chef. It tastes even better than it looks."

"I'm glad you like it," Javier said. "I'll tell Marcos. He's thinking about adding it to the menu."

"Speaking of Marcos, how are things going with him? Are Wendy and the baby doing well?"

"Yes, they're all great. Apparently, Mary Anne is thriving and gaining weight. I haven't seen her yet, so I'm looking forward to visiting them soon."

"Mary Anne's a cutie," Leah said. "I went to the NICU a couple of times and saw her through the window. I know your family was worried about her for a while, so it's nice that she's home now and doing well."

"I hadn't realized you checked on her, but I'm glad you did."

Leah smiled. "I don't always get that close to a patient's family, but in your case, it was easy to do. Your dad is a great guy. And your brothers and sister are nice, too. In fact after hearing so much about Wendy and their concern for her, I went to the maternity ward a few times to visit with her and to give her a report on your progress. Then, after the baby was born, I stopped by the NICU to take a peek at her."

Javier seemed to ponder that for a while, then said, "Wendy and Marcos are hosting an open house on Friday. Why don't you come with me? You'd get a chance to see my family again. The baby, too."

Leah hadn't mentioned that she'd visited the neonatal unit nearly every day after Mary Anne's birth, just for a chance to look at the tiny babies, to watch the mommies and daddies peering into isolettes, reaching in and stroking a tiny foot or hand.

She'd like to see Mary Anne, now that she was healthy and at home. She'd been so tiny, so fragile at birth. Yet so precious, too.

But more than that, attending the party meant that Leah would see Javier again.

Afraid to tip her hand, to reveal her yearning, she said, "I don't know. I'm not a family member, so I'd hate to intrude on a special celebration."

"My family knows how helpful and supportive you've been to me, as well as to them during my hospitalization. And they think of you as a friend. I know they'd be happy to see you there."

What about Javier? Would he be happy to have her there with him? Was that why he was including her?

"I'll think about it." Yet even as the vague, noncommittal words rolled off her tongue, she realized that, deep inside, she actually wanted to go.

She'd always enjoyed being around loving families since she really hadn't had one of her own. In fact, sometimes she wondered if getting married and having children was even in her future. Her own experience as a child, as well as her two attempts at having a romantic relationship as an adult, had resulted in one disillusion after another.

Maybe that's why it was so easy to remain dedicated to her patients. Nursing provided her with an opportunity to nurture others almost daily without risking disappointment and heartbreak.

She stole a glance at Javier, watched him cut into his chicken and take a bite. She'd better focus on the meal in front of her, rather than on dreams that might never come true.

When they finished eating, Javier pushed aside his plate and tossed her a smile. "How about some ice cream? I've got chocolate and strawberry to choose from. And even some raspberry sherbet."

She hadn't left much room for dessert, but she wasn't in any hurry to leave just yet. So she said, "A little sherbet sounds good. Why don't you stay seated? I'll get it. Just tell me which flavor you want."

"Thanks. I'll have the chocolate."

When Leah returned and placed his bowl in front of him, he thanked her again, then added, "I don't usually expect people to wait on me."

"Don't give it another thought. I don't mind at all."
Leah took her seat and dug into her sherbet, relishing
the sweet, tangy raspberry taste.

As she dipped her spoon in for a second bite, she
asked, "What's the first thing you want to do when
you're discharged completely?"

"Besides taking you out on the town?"

She smiled, wondering if he really planned to ask
her out. Sure, he'd said that he wanted to. But what
if he turned out to be as insincere as the lawyer who
dumped Aunt Connie and broke her heart?

Leah had nearly fallen for a man like that once,
and she'd been determined to avoid playboy bachelors
ever since.

Would Javier prove to be different from the man
she suspected he'd been before the accident?

She hoped so, because a failed romance with Javier
would be a lot harder to bounce back from than either
of the two relationships she'd had in the past.

Of course, she hadn't invested all that much emo-
tion in them, and she found herself caring for Javier
a little more each day.

While finishing their dessert, they made small talk
for a while. Then, when both bowls were empty, Leah
stood to clear the table.

"Don't bother doing the dishes. Margarita's coming
again tomorrow, and I want her to have plenty to keep
her busy."

He'd told her the same thing last time, but just like before, Leah refused to let his housekeeper clean up after her—no matter how badly Javier wanted to provide the older woman with work.

Fortunately, they'd had takeout, so there weren't any pots and pans to wash or countertops to be wiped down. She merely had to fill the sink with soapy water, then she compromised again by leaving the dishes to soak.

When she returned to the dining room, Javier was just getting to his feet. A grimace on his face let her know that it had been a long day and probably a painful one.

"Don't get up," she said. "I can see myself out."

He seemed to rally and lobbed a boyish grin her way. "Just like making sure I saved room for dessert, I managed to save enough energy to walk you to the door."

She returned his smile, wondering if he had plans to kiss her again. While it probably wasn't a good idea, she decided not to put up a fight if he made a move in that direction.

As they walked through the living room, she stopped to pick up her purse. Then they headed to the door.

"Thanks again for dinner," she said. "It was a nice treat."

"I'll have to grill for you someday."

There he went again with the "someday" talk. Why

did he seem to put everything off to the future? Why not give her an actual date to look forward to—like next Saturday or even three weeks from whenever?

She had no idea, other than to think he wanted to take things slowly, and that was probably for the best.

As she opened the front door and stepped out on the stoop, he stopped her with a question.

"Are you working on Friday?"

"No, I've got the weekend off. Why?"

"Because I won't have to wait until seven to pick you up. I'll come for you around six."

"Where are we going?"

"To Marcos and Wendy's house."

She was about to remind him that she'd said she would think about going, but maybe he could read her a lot better than she'd thought he could. Either way, she wasn't going to fight him on the party.

"All right," she said. "I'll be ready."

She gave him her address although he didn't write it down.

He nodded and his eyes glimmered. "I'll see you then."

Apparently so.

But before she could turn to go, he slipped his free arm around her waist and drew her toward him.

Her heart rate spiked as anticipation soared.

Only a fool would turn down a kiss from Javier

Mendoza. So she wrapped her arms around his neck and leaned toward him.

As his lips touched hers, she was lost in a burst of fireworks, this time even better than the last.

Chapter Nine

Four long days had passed since Javier kissed Leah on the porch and set the stars spinning, yet not an hour went by without her thinking about his lips pressed on hers, his tongue sweeping the inside of her mouth, seeking hers for a lovers' tryst.

She'd tried to attribute her mindless arousal to the fact that she'd been suppressing her physical needs and desires. After all, it had been ages since she'd felt a man's embrace. But the truth was, until she'd met Javier, she hadn't obsessed about sex at all. So there was only one explanation that made sense. Now that she'd had a taste of what was to come, what she would experience in his slow, expert hands, she hungered for more.

She hadn't talked to him since that night at his house, and when Friday finally rolled around, she'd spent the afternoon fixing her hair—putting it up, then leaving it down. After getting dressed and applying her makeup, she settled on wearing a soft and feminine look.

As it grew close to six o'clock, the time Javier was supposed to arrive, she reminded herself that attending the open house wouldn't be a date. It was only a chance for her to see the Mendoza family again and to wish Wendy, Marcos and the baby her best.

But she wasn't so sure about that. Not when she was looking forward to seeing Javier again, to being with him.

When the doorbell rang, she took one last look in the mirror, then went to answer the door.

"Wow," Javier said, his eyes lighting up with appreciation. "You look great, Leah. I've been waiting to see your hair down and loose."

"Thanks. You look nice, too."

His hair, which was still growing out, had been trimmed and styled. He'd also shaved and splashed on some woodsy cologne that set her senses reeling. She didn't recognize the brand or the scent, but it was no doubt as expensive as it was alluring.

He wore a light blue button-down shirt, open at the collar, and a pair of black slacks with a matching jacket. He seemed so strong, so vital, so whole, that anyone who was unaware of what he'd suffered, what he'd been through, would think the cane was only a prop.

"Are you ready to go?" he asked.

"Yes." She locked the door, then walked with him to his SUV.

Less than ten minutes later, Javier pulled along the curb and parked in front of Marcos and Wendy's modest three-bedroom house.

"It doesn't look like anyone's here yet," he said, scanning the street and the driveway. "But that's bound to change soon."

"Are they expecting a lot of people?" Leah asked.

"If you'd ever attended a Mendoza get-together, you'd realize what a big family I have. And when you add the Fortunes from Red Rock, as well as those from Atlanta, well…" He grinned. "There will probably be a slew of them, but with it being an open house, people will be coming and going all evening."

Leah and Javier climbed from the car, then made their way to the front door, where Marcos welcomed them.

"Are we the first ones here?" Javier asked.

"Yes, unless you count Emily, Wendy's sister."

From what Leah had heard, Emily Fortune had flown in from Atlanta to help care for the baby. It must be nice to have a sister, she thought, especially at times like this.

At that moment, the new mommy entered the living room wearing a brightly colored gypsy skirt and a matching red top, as well as a full apron to protect the fabric from kitchen spills and splatters.

Wendy welcomed Javier with a hug, then turned and embraced Leah as well. "I'm so glad y'all are here."

"Thanks for inviting me to tag along," Leah said.

"I would have been disappointed if you hadn't. You have no idea how much I appreciated your visits while I was in the hospital. You not only kept me in the loop, letting me know about Javier's condition, you also helped me feel better about my own situation."

"It was my pleasure," Leah said. "How's the baby? It must be wonderful to finally have her home."

"She's doing great. I'll take you to see her in the nursery. Emily's changing her diaper."

Wendy led Leah through the living room, which was an eclectic mix of a contemporary style with a bit of cozy chic added here and there. From what she'd been told, Wendy was a fashionista, and it showed both in her clothing and her house.

"I like your decor," Leah said.

"Thanks." Wendy chuckled. "I did what I could with what Marcos had. This place used to be a bachelor pad, with lots of leather and chrome that centered around a big-screen TV. But I added my own little touches here and there, and this is what we ended up with."

"Well, I'm impressed. You certainly did an amazing job."

"Thanks." Wendy led Leah down the hall, stopping near an open doorway. "Here it is."

Leah peered into the nursery, where Emily Fortune stood at the changing table with the tiny baby who was still the size of a small newborn.

"Have you met my sister?" Wendy asked.

"Yes, several times." Leah smiled at Emily. "It's nice to see you again."

Emily laughed. "I'd shake your hand, but I'm a little tied up at the moment."

"I can see that." Leah eased into the room.

"Well, if you two don't mind," Wendy said, nodding toward the hallway, "I have something in the oven and need to check on it."

After Wendy took off down the hall, Leah scanned the nursery, with its white walls and furniture. The curtains, a tropical fabric with fuchsia, orange and lemon-yellow flowers on a bright aqua background, as well as a hand-painted border with the same floral print, added a blast of color to the room.

And so did a white glider and ottoman upholstered in a matching bright aqua.

"The nursery is darling," Leah said. "Your sister has a real talent with decor."

"Yes, she does. She's becoming a real domestic goddess." Emily Fortune, the oldest of the Atlanta Fortune daughters, was the director of advertising for FortuneSouth Enterprises.

At five foot seven, with long blond hair and green

eyes, Emily had a sophisticated air about her—maybe due in part to the glasses she often wore.

Leah had thought of her as a career woman, but standing here in the nursery, changing a newborn's diaper, gave her a whole different look.

"I'm just about done here," Emily said as she put a second little foot into the pink sleeper. "And once this last snap is done, I'll let you hold her if you'd like."

"I'd love to," Leah said.

After taking the baby, Leah sat in the rocker and began to glide back and forth while Emily looked on with a loving smile.

From what Leah had heard, Emily had been buried alive during the tornado. But unlike Javier, she'd come out without any serious injuries.

Leah studied the baby in her arms. "She's precious. And while she's still small, she's a lot bigger than when she was in the neonatal intensive care unit."

"She's hungry all the time," Emily added. "I have a feeling she'll be outgrowing her preemie clothes in no time at all."

Leah reached for the child's small foot, felt her little toes inside the pretty pink sleeper. She'd worked in the NICU briefly after she'd graduated from nursing school, so she'd handled preemies. But this was different. Mary Anne was healthy and thriving.

"You look good with a baby in your arms," Emily said. "If Javier saw you like that, he'd be in awe—and undoubtedly thinking about the future."

Leah cocked her head slightly. "What do you mean?"

"Rumor has it that there might be another Mendoza wedding one of these days."

Seriously? Was Emily talking about *Javier?*

And *Leah?*

What did she mean by "rumor"? Where would anyone get an idea like that? After all, Leah wasn't even sure what she and Javier were dancing around.

"I can't imagine how a rumor like that might get started," Leah finally said. "It's way too early in our friendship to even think about something so far off as marriage. Besides, Javier has lived the life of a happy bachelor for years. I'm not so sure he'll ever want to settle down."

"I don't know about that," Emily said. "I've always been career focused, even when I was a freshman in high school. But being in a tornado, fearing for my life, has made me reevaluate a lot of things."

Leah could see where a near-death experience could open a person's eyes. Is that what was going on with Javier? Was he actually reexamining his life and planning to make some changes, too?

She hoped so.

Mary Anne began to squirm, to scrunch up her tiny face and fuss.

"What's the matter?" Leah asked. "Do you think she's hungry?"

"Actually, Wendy just fed her a few minutes ago. Maybe she needs to burp."

As Mary Anne continued to cry, Leah put her up on her shoulder and began to pat her back to no avail.

"Let me give it a try," Emily said, taking the baby from Leah. She paced the nursery floor, patting the child's back lightly.

Moments later, as a burp sounded, Mary Anne stopped her fussing and settled down. Once she was quiet and still, Emily handed her back to Leah, taking time to stroke her little cheek, to look at her with love and longing.

"I imagine being around this precious baby makes a woman wish she could get married and start a family of her own," Leah said.

"Yes, I'll admit that it makes motherhood appealing. But I'm not thinking about marriage. I've given up waiting for Mr. Right to come along. What I really want is to have a baby."

Leah liked the idea, too. But she'd nearly given up on having a child, on becoming a mother.

"My brother, Blake, inspired me to come up with a plan to make it happen," Emily said.

"A plan?"

"Yes, and it's a good one. I compiled a spreadsheet of fertility clinics with their success rate percentages, as well as a list of exclusive sperm banks that use only Ivy League, Mensa and Nobel Prize–winning donors.

I also have the names of several well-recommended adoption attorneys who promise fast results."

Leah didn't know what to say about that. Talk about coming up with a family plan and seeing it to fruition....

Still, as much as Leah might like to have a little one of her own, she'd rather conceive a baby the old-fashioned way.

With that thought came a vision of her and Javier, stretched out in bed together, naked and kissing and stroking...

Whoa. Talk about inappropriate times and places.

Leah quickly squelched the amazing, blood-stirring thought and returned her attention to the baby in her arms.

"Emily?" Marcos called from the doorway. When both women looked up, he said, "Wendy would like your help with something in the kitchen."

"I'll be right there." Emily reached down and caressed the baby's head, running her hand along the soft tufts of dark hair. Then she excused herself, leaving Leah alone with the baby.

Emily hadn't been gone long when Leah sensed someone watching her. When she glanced up, she spotted Javier in the doorway, a wistful smile on his face.

For a moment, something bound them together—a thought, a look, an unspoken dream.

Or had searching his expression while she held

a baby in her arms set her imagination off on a tangent, seeking a pot of gold at the end of a rainbow that didn't exist?

Leah tamped down her musing, which was probably a result of the "rumors" Emily had mentioned. But that didn't mean she could ignore the fact that Javier stood in the doorway, looking at her in a way that touched her very core.

Javier had been so blown away by the sight of Leah holding a baby, so amazed to see the maternal side of her that he'd stood in the doorway, unable to move or to speak.

"Have you met your niece yet?" she asked.

"No, but I'd like to." Still, it took him a moment to make that first step, to cross the carpeted nursery floor with his cane in hand. But once he did, he peered at his brother's firstborn baby, nearly dumbstruck with awe.

"Do you want to hold her?" Leah asked.

"No, I'll just look at her. She's so tiny. And I'm not very good on my feet yet. I'd hate to drop her."

"You can have my chair."

"Please don't get up."

Leah looked so good like that, rocking a sleeping newborn. She was going to make one heck of a mother; he was sure of it.

When the doorbell rang and voices sounded in the

living room, Javier realized that the other guests had begun to arrive.

"Looks like the open house is finally getting under way," he said.

"Then I'd better take Mary Anne to her mommy and daddy." Leah carefully got to her feet. "I need to let someone else hold her for a while."

Javier took a step back, even though he hated to see Leah leave the nursery. Seeing her with a child in her arms—so serene, so loving—was enough to make him wonder what she'd look like holding a baby of her own.

His baby.

But Javier wouldn't allow himself to have those kinds of thoughts before he could comfortably walk the floor with a fussy baby, take a toddler to the park or show a boy how to ride a bike or hit a baseball.

A *boy?*

Somehow, that didn't seem to matter. If he were to have a daughter, he'd teach her how to do those things, too.

With Leah on her feet, he took the time to get a closer look at his brother's newborn, the tiny angel who'd come to bless their lives.

"I can see a lot of Wendy in her," he said. "But she's got my brother's eyes. She's beautiful, isn't she?"

"Absolutely."

As they reached the doorway, Javier let Leah and

the baby go first, then he followed them into the living room, where the Atlanta Fortunes had gathered.

He greeted Wendy's brother Blake and his fiancée, Katie Wallace, first. Then he took the time to introduce the couple to Leah.

Blake, who was the head of marketing for FortuneSouth Enterprises, and Katie had been childhood friends. She'd been in love with him for years, and the two had recently become engaged.

Javier's mother, if she were still alive, would have announced that love was in the air. And maybe she would have been right, because next in line for introductions was Wendy's brother Scott and his fiancée, Christina Hastings.

Scott, the vice president of FourtuneSouth Enterprises, had been trapped with Christina during the tornado. And within the first few weeks in January, he and the pretty waitress had fallen in love.

Leah, who'd met the couple while Javier had been in the hospital, greeted them.

By the time Javier got around to introducing Wendy's parents, Virginia Alice and John Michael, everyone had gathered around Leah, who still held Mary Anne.

"I think it's time for her grandmother to take her," Leah said, handing over the baby to the silver-haired woman.

Virginia Alice beamed as she took the child,

clearly thrilled to see her newest grandbaby again, this time without all the NICU monitors attached.

Leah took a step back, getting out of the way of the crowd, and Javier couldn't blame her for that. There were a lot of people in the room, and even more would be passing through the door this evening.

Still, she'd handled it well, greeting each of them with grace and style. But he'd make an excuse to leave pretty soon. Once they'd had a drink and eaten a couple of the appetizers Wendy had made, Javier would tell everyone he was tired. Then he and Leah could escape.

Just the thought of having her to himself again brought a smile to his face.

As the women continued to coo over the baby, Javier turned to John Michael, the patriarch of the Atlanta Fortunes. "When did you get in?"

"Just a few hours ago. Scott picked us up at the airport, then drove us to his and Christina's place."

Marcos had mentioned that Scott and Christina had a seven-bedroom home, so there had to be plenty of room for guests.

"Would anyone like a drink?" Marcos asked his guests. "I have a bar set up in the patio."

"I'll take you up on that." John Michael patted his son-in-law on the back, then followed him out of the living room.

At six feet four inches and with salt-and-pepper hair, John Michael was not only distinguished, but imposing as well. Javier suspected a lot of that had to do with the fact that he'd created FortuneSouth Enterprises, a huge telecommunications company, and had become a millionaire by the time he was thirty.

He was sixty-two now and had only refined his blunt, aggressive approach to both business and life.

He and his wife had been married for nearly forty years, although Javier suspected she deserved a lot of credit for holding down the home front while he commandeered the business.

Virginia Alice was the epitome of a genteel, Southern woman—an authentic steel magnolia. She was also as soft-spoken as her husband was blunt.

From what Marcos had told Javier, the woman had raised their six children single-handedly and didn't believe in nannies.

Jordana, Wendy's sister, was the last to step through the threshold, and when Javier tried to introduce the two women, Leah said, "We met one day at the hospital. It's good to see you again, Jordana."

"Yes, it is."

"The last time we talked," Leah said, "you were getting ready to fly back to Atlanta."

"And now I'm back." Jordana smiled. "I couldn't miss this party—and a chance to see my niece again."

Jordana Fortune, the assistant director of research and development for FortuneSouth Enterprises, was a bright woman with blond hair and brown eyes. She also had a shy demeanor.

Javier shot a glance at Leah, saw that she was holding her own with the ladies, so he said, "I'll be back shortly. Can I bring you a drink?"

"A diet soda, if they have one."

Javier nodded, then followed the men out to the patio. He was looking forward to having a quick drink with his friends and family. Then he would take Leah back home, where he planned to kiss her one more time.

And maybe take things a little further than that...

Leah doubted that she'd be able to keep all the Fortunes straight, but at least she knew Javier's family from having seen them regularly at the hospital.

Luis had been the first Mendoza to arrive, followed by Rafe and Melina.

Apparently Isabella had an art show of some kind today. From what Leah had been told, Isabella and J.R. would definitely attend the open house, but they'd be arriving late.

After taking time to chat with Javier's father and siblings, Leah scanned the small but cozy living room and found herself envying the close-knit group. Javier might complain about his siblings at times, but it was clear that they all loved and supported each other.

The Fortunes, too, for better or worse, seemed closely involved in one another's lives. And for a moment, Leah tried to imagine having a family like that.

And having a husband like Javier.

She'd seen him with the baby, watched him with his friends and siblings. Had she been wrong about him being a Casanova?

There was so much she had yet to learn about the man, so much she wanted to learn.

Before she knew it, he was at her side.

"Are you ready to go?"

She wouldn't mind staying a while longer or leaving, but she suspected he was getting tired. So she said, "I'm ready whenever you are."

"I think we've stayed long enough."

Leah stood, then said her goodbyes to the hosts, as well as the people she'd met. Everyone seemed glad that she'd come with Javier and sorry that they had to leave, but they understood.

What they didn't realize—and Leah did—was that she was actually looking forward to the drive home and spending some quiet time with Javier. She might even invite him into her house for a cup of coffee or whatever else he might want.

Her thoughts took another sexual turn, and she tried to shake them off. It's not as though their relationship had progressed beyond a good-night kiss.

As Leah and Javier left the house, they spotted Jordana Fortune standing just off the porch, looking a little green around the gills.

"Are you okay?" Leah asked.

The woman nodded. "Yes, I'm fine. It was just a little warm and crowded in there."

"You don't look fine," Javier said. "Maybe you should go inside and lie down."

"No, I don't want to go back in the house."

"Maybe you should let Leah look at you," Javier said, as he leaned against his cane. "You might need to see a doctor."

"I'm fine," Jordana said. *"Really."* Her gaze quickly sought Leah's. "It's nothing contagious. And it'll pass soon."

It didn't take much of a leap for Leah to realize that Jordana might be pregnant.

"Would you like me to get you some saltines? Or maybe some ginger ale?"

"That might help. But please don't mention that it's for me. Or that you saw me out here, okay?"

Realizing that her assumption might prove to be right, Leah nodded. "If there's one thing I've learned how to do since becoming a nurse, it's to be discreet. This will be our little secret."

Leah glanced at Javier, indicating that he was in on the secret, too. And while she didn't think he'd come to the same conclusion she had, he nodded in agreement.

Moments later, Leah returned outside with the soft drink and crackers, only to find Javier out near the street, talking to J.R. and Isabella, who'd just arrived.

Jordana had moved, too. Now she stood near the tree at the side of the house, talking to someone on her cell phone.

Leah wasn't sure if she should stand back, giving the woman her privacy, or let her know she'd returned. As it was, she drew closer, only to catch a bit of conversation.

"What do you mean I'm not the only one with unfinished business in Red Rock?" Jordana asked.

Leah's steps froze. Surely this was a conversation she wasn't meant to hear. So she turned to walk away, just as Jordana said, "How do you plan to make things right, Victoria?" She paused. "Okay. Then I'll wait in Red Rock until you fly in."

As Leah reached the porch, Javier returned with J.R. and Isabella. The couples greeted each other, making the typical small talk, then the Fortunes entered the house.

Javier looked at the drink and crackers in Leah's hand. "Where's Jordana?"

"She's over there." Leah nodded toward the tree.

"What's she doing?"

"She's on her cell phone, talking with someone named Victoria."

"Her cousin?"

"I suppose so. As soon as she hangs up, I'll give her the soda and crackers. Then we can go home."

Moments later, Jordana returned to the porch, looking just as pale and nauseous as she'd been before— maybe even more so.

Something told Leah the conversation with Victoria had upset Jordana, but she wasn't about to pry into someone else's business. Besides, Javier had been on his feet long enough today. And she was eager to go home, where the two of them would be alone.

And where she might kiss him again.

Chapter Ten

It was almost eight o'clock when Leah and Javier finally left the party and headed back to her house.

After parking in the driveway, Javier opened the driver's door.

"You don't have to get out," Leah said. "Unless you want to. I know how tired you must be. It's been a busy day for you."

"I'm fine."

They climbed from his SUV and made their way to the front door, the porch light illuminating their path along the sidewalk.

Leah had been fighting a growing attraction to Javier ever since she'd first laid eyes on him in his hospital bed. As long as he'd been on the third floor and under her care, she'd refused to even consider becoming romantically involved with a patient, which was a matter of ethics. But now that he'd been discharged, that was no longer a reason to hold back.

Okay, so he was still technically under the care of San Antonio General as an outpatient at the attached rehab facility. But she could easily argue that it wasn't the same thing. And that it wouldn't be a violation of any kind.

Next she'd worried about him being a player, a perpetual bachelor who had no plans to ever get married or to settle down. But she now had evidence to dispute that belief, too.

Either way, she'd come to the conclusion that her feelings for Javier had grown too strong to fight. And that she'd already lost the battle.

By the time they reached her front door, her heart soared with anticipation.

Yet she couldn't help noting that Javier had been walking slower than before.

Was he reluctant to say goodbye to her and end their night together?

Or had he pushed himself too hard and grown tired at the party?

As she reached for her key, she asked, "Would you like to come in? I can make us some tea or coffee. I also have some soft drinks and a bottle of wine."

"Decaf sounds good if you have it."

"I do." She let him inside, then closed the door

and turned on the light. Everything was just as she'd left it. Even Miss Kitty was still snoozing on the blue chintz love seat, her favorite resting spot.

The cat looked up, but only for a moment. Apparently the old gray tabby didn't care that Leah had brought home a guest. But then again, at her age, she didn't worry much as long as she had a little peace and quiet.

"Why don't you have a seat while I brew a pot of decaf," Leah said.

"All right."

She left Javier in the living room, then made her way to the kitchen, where she filled the carafe with water. As she shut off the faucet, she heard music playing—something soft, slow and seductive.

Was he trying to set up a romantic ambiance while they ended their evening together? A part of her hoped that he was. But she doubted that was the case.

Javier had to be exhausted. And since he'd told her that music relaxed him, he was probably trying to unwind after an afternoon at rehab and an evening spent at his brother's open house.

Yet as Leah finished placing the coffee grounds into the filter-lined basket and turned on the power to start the brewing process, she couldn't help wondering what awaited her in the other part of the house— even if it was just a tall, dark and handsome man stretched out on her sofa.

While the water gurgled and dribbled into the pot,

she returned to the living room, only to find Javier seated on her love seat next to Miss Kitty. He stroked the cat, who seemed rather indifferent about having company. But at least she wasn't hissing at him.

"I hope you don't mind that I put on some music," he said. "It was pretty quiet in here, and your cat wasn't much company."

She smiled. "That's not surprising. Miss Kitty is nearly nineteen years old, so she's content to sleep most of the day and night. And no, I don't mind the music at all."

Still, she wasn't sure what had compelled him to choose that particular radio station. Did it have anything to do with the romantic ballad that was playing?

She listened to the lyrics for a moment, as well as the sound of a lonely fiddle, then said, "I like this song."

"I do, too. Why don't we dance to it?"

His question came as a complete surprise, and while she thought it was a nice idea, he had to be worn out from the day's activities.

"How are you feeling?" she asked. "Are you really up to it?"

"Probably not." He tossed her a boyish grin as he slowly got to his feet, biting back a grimace. "But the way I see it, if I drop in my tracks, I'm with the right person. You'll know just what to do."

He took a step away from the sofa, letting the cane

lean against the armrest. Then he held out his arms in an invitation to give it a whirl.

"This probably isn't a very good idea," Leah said, mindful of the severity of his injuries, of the long road he had to full recovery. Yet she still made her way toward him.

"No need to worry about me," he said. "I have it all figured out."

She couldn't see any reason to argue or to point out his weakness, so she stepped into his embrace, leaned her body into his and offered her support.

The woodsy scent of his cologne mingled with the pheromones overhead, creating an arousing spell that was too strong to resist. So she placed her cheek against his chest, relishing the warmth of his body, the steady beat of his heart.

Did he feel it, too—the sexual thrill, the rush of desire, the longing for more than an embrace?

They swayed to the music, although they didn't actually dance. Yet that didn't matter. All Leah wanted to do was to hold Javier close for as long as she had the chance.

When the song ended, he continued to sway on his feet, then dipped slightly. She held him tight, determined to support him, to keep him steady and upright.

Was he in pain? Was his strength giving out?

Or had a stumble been part of a plan to gain her sympathy, to weaken her defenses, to get her into bed?

Oh, for heaven's sake. Enough of that already. Not every handsome, eligible bachelor was a playboy whose only goal was to score.

Leah took a step back, intending to retrieve Javier's cane so he could support himself better, so he could make his way back to the love seat. But before she could turn away, he caught her chin with his finger, then tilted her face upward.

She saw the kiss coming in his eyes, felt it in the pounding of her heart. As their mouths met, their lips parted and the kiss deepened, just as though their bodies knew right where they'd left off. Only this time, the intimacy of it all intensified as their hands explored, stroked and caressed until Leah could scarcely breathe.

When Javier's hand reached her breast, when he palmed the soft mound, he skimmed his thumb across her nipple—once, twice, a third time.

Her breath caught and her senses spun out of control.

The man was a master when it came to romance—the absolute best. And while she knew she ought to be leery of him, her desire and curiosity mounted until she wanted nothing more than to learn what she was going to experience in his arms next.

Kissing Javier suddenly seemed to be the best decision she'd ever made—or *not* made, since her brain was no longer in charge of her actions.

As he worked his magic with his hands, his mouth

and tongue, an ache settled low in her core, reminding her of just how long it had been since she'd had sex, how empty she'd become. And that sweet ache merely grew until her head swam and her knees threatened to buckle.

But no way could she allow herself to become unsteady on her feet. If that happened, she might not be able to keep Javier from falling if the need arose.

So she drew her lips from his, knowing she was doing the best and wisest thing, even though every cell in her body screamed out in complaint.

"I need to get off my feet," she said, rather than admit that her real concern was for him. Javier, like most men, probably wouldn't like having his weakness pointed out.

"Do you want to take a seat?" he asked. "Or maybe...lie down?"

Javier clearly knew how to wine and dine and charm a woman into bed. Yet Leah would throw caution aside and listen to her hormones—just this once.

"The sofa could get awkward," she said. "Maybe we should go into my room and stretch out on the bed."

When Javier didn't answer right away, she feared she'd gotten the wrong message.

Had she misunderstood his intentions?

Javier could hardly believe what Leah had just agreed to, and while he ought to backpedal on the whole let's-take-this-to-the-bedroom thing, it was too late to do that now. Everything he needed to make love—his libido, his hormones, his erection—had escaped injury in the tornado. So he was primed and ready for love.

"Lying down sounds like a good idea to me," he said.

As Leah stooped to reach for the discarded cane, a kindness on her part that reminded Javier that she was well aware of his physical shortcomings, his gut clenched.

He remembered the decision he'd made to maintain a platonic relationship with her until he'd fully recovered. But what was he supposed to do? Turn around and limp away?

Let her see how far he still had to go before making a full recovery?

But he had one thing going for him—his skill as a lover. And that was something the tornado hadn't stolen from him.

After that last kiss he and Leah had shared, after those amazing moments of foreplay, he was willing to change his game plan at this point. After all, the rest of his body might be struggling to walk without the aid of a cane, but there were certain parts of him that worked just fine—especially if he would be lying down.

He might not be able to make her any promises about the future, but there was one thing he knew for sure. He was going to do everything in his power to make things good for her tonight. And, if all went as he hoped they would, he would take her to a sexual place no other man had ever taken her before.

As Leah led Javier to the bedroom, he followed her, convinced he was doing the right thing. And thanking his lucky stars that he'd been in the habit of carrying a condom with him.

Once they reached her bed, he kissed her again. Then after he kicked off his loafers, he looked to her for either approval or objection.

Damn. Where had the doubt come from?

But it didn't last long. As she slipped out of her heels, he knew they were on the same page.

He took off his black sports coat and, after removing the condom he kept in the inside pocket, he draped the jacket over the bedpost. Then he left the foil packet on the nightstand.

The seconds ticked slowly as they continued to undress, one garment at a time.

She lifted the hem of her top, then pulled it over her head and let it drop to the floor.

He unbuttoned his shirt, then moved on to the cuffs. All the while, sometimes out of the corner of his eye and at others straight on, he watched every seductive movement she made, following her step by step.

She undid the button on her slacks, then tugged

down the zipper. When she was done, she peeled the black fabric over her hips, then wiggled out of them.

He removed his pants as well.

All the while their eyes remained on each other, watching, gazing with both longing and appreciation.

When they'd finally discarded their clothing and stood before each other naked, her pure beauty struck him hard and low.

"I had no idea how beautiful you really are."

She thanked him as if she didn't quite believe him but was too polite to argue. He was going to have to do something about that. And the first step was to take her in his arms again, to let her feel his skin on hers. As her breasts pressed against his chest, he kissed her like there was no tomorrow.

Sure, they'd have to face the consequences of their actions after the night was over, but he wasn't going to think about any of that now.

His hands slid along the curve of her back, then down the slopes of her hips. As he drew her close, a surge of desire shot right through him.

When he doubted that his once-broken legs could hold out much longer, he ended the kiss, nodded toward the bed and said, "After you."

She drew back the covers, then climbed onto the mattress. As much as he wanted to join her, he couldn't help taking in the sight of her as she lay naked and lovely.

Her legs were long and shapely, her breasts full,

her nipples peaked. Her eyes watching him with as much appreciation as he watched her.

They'd kissed off the last of her lipstick, leaving her lips red and plump. And with her head on the pillows, those long, glossy strands of auburn hair were splayed against the white cotton pillowcase—just as he'd imagined so many times before.

Unable to hold off a moment longer, he slid into bed beside her. And as they lay together, he kissed her again—this time with all the hunger, all the passion rushing through his veins.

She whimpered, then arched forward, revealing her own need, her own arousal.

As she skimmed her nails across his chest, sending a shiver through him and a surge of heat zipping through his veins, he knew he couldn't prolong their first joining indefinitely.

But that didn't mean he wouldn't take the time to kiss her breasts until she was begging to have him fill her to the brim.

So he leaned over her and took the first dusky pink tip into his mouth.

Leah gasped in pleasure, yet Javier continued to taunt her, to make her yearn for more. Then he turned his attention to the other side until she gripped his arms, making crescent dents into his skin with her nails.

"I'm not sure how much more of this I can take,"

she said. "I need you inside me or I'm going to scream."

A smile stretched across his face. "When that happens, you just might cry out in pleasure anyway."

Her smile turned sultry, then she reached for the condom on the nightstand and tore into it. When she'd helped him roll it in place, he turned to the side and hovered over her.

At this very moment in time, there was no place else he longed to be, no one else he wanted to be with. And he was sorely tempted to tell her so.

While the unspoken words stalled in his throat, words he'd never uttered to another woman in his life, he did his best to choke them back. It was too soon to utter promises he wasn't quite ready to make.

But one thing was certain. Javier belonged to Leah—at least for tonight.

As she opened for him, he entered her slowly, deliberately, relishing the experience of two lovers becoming one for the first time.

And as her body responded to his, as she arched up to meet each of his thrusts, he couldn't recall anyone else ever taking him to such a soaring height.

Hell, he couldn't even remember any other lover's name. And for some reason, he doubted that he ever would again.

When he reached a peak, she arched up, dug her nails into his back and cried out with her climax, setting off one of his own.

They came together, as a blast of colors burst somewhere in his mind, and he held her tight until the last sexual wave eased.

He wanted to speak, to again tell her how beautiful she was, how good they were together, how much he...

Damn. It was way, *way* too early to mutter emotions best left alone until he was back to normal, until he had a chance to determine if they were really true, if what he felt right this moment might actually last.

But double damn. Making love with Leah had been awesome, amazing and...unreal.

Javier might not be anywhere near one hundred percent physically, but tell that to his libido, which still worked like a charm. Tonight he'd been on top of his sexual game.

Still, he had no idea where the relationship would go from here.

As it was, he'd sleep on it until dawn's first light. Maybe then he'd have an idea about what he wanted to do about this.

He'd always considered himself doing a solo gig in life, and up until now, it had worked out just fine. And while the injuries he'd suffered in the tornado had set him back for months, they'd also opened his eyes to a lot of things.

For the first time in his life, he could imagine himself settling down and having a family. But not now. Not until he was back on his feet without the aid of a cane. Not until he'd gone back to work at the office and had a couple of deals cooking.

Not until he could shoot par at the Red Rock Country Club again.

Not until he knew he was number one.

Sure, he knew he could spill his guts, share his fears about all of that with Leah and he knew she'd tell him that she liked him just the way he was.

But Javier didn't like himself. And he wasn't going to let an awesome night of lovemaking convince him that he'd be number one again at everything he tackled.

So instead of saying anything at all to Leah and tipping his hand, he held her close, afraid to let her go.

Or to face whatever reality the morning brought.

Chapter Eleven

The rising sun peered through the spaces in the shutter slats and cast dawn's muted light in Leah's room, where she lay in bed, more asleep than awake.

She'd just spent the most incredible night of her life with Javier, who'd proven to be an amazing lover, even better than in her dreams. And she looked forward to what the new day would bring.

So she reached for him, hoping to stroke his arm and whisper good morning. But the only thing she touched was the cool expanse of mattress and a rumpled sheet.

At first she thought that he was in the bathroom, but she didn't hear any water running.

Where was he?

Surely he hadn't slipped away in the middle of the night. She sat up in bed, scanned the faintly lit room and spotted her discarded clothes lying in a pile on the floor.

But Javier's weren't anywhere to be seen.

Her heart dropped to her stomach with a cold, hard thump—until she took a whiff and caught the aroma of fresh-brewed coffee.

Was he fixing breakfast for her?

She ought to be the one in the kitchen, cooking for him—not the other way around. He was her guest, and an injured one at that. So she threw off the covers, climbed from the bed and removed her pink chenille robe from the closet. Then she padded into the kitchen where, sure enough, he stood near the stove, his cane leaning against the counter, his jacket hung over the back of a chair.

His hair was damp and stylishly mussed as he lifted the lid of the frying pan and peered into whatever he had cooking in it.

"Good morning," she said. "You're up early."

He turned and smiled. "Yeah, well I couldn't sleep. So I showered. And since neither of us had much for dinner last night, I thought I'd come in here and whip up some scrambled eggs. You didn't have bacon, but I found some red potatoes and English muffins. I hope that's okay."

"It's fine." In fact, it was great. Not only was he a good lover, but he knew his way around a kitchen.

He was also thoughtful. If he'd already showered and dressed, he must have gone out of his way to keep quiet.

She appreciated his consideration, until she imagined him as a bachelor again, with more women coming in and out of his life than he could count. And if that were the case, then he'd probably had a lot of practice getting out of bed quietly and slipping away in the middle of the night.

But the moment that thought arose, she tamped it down and scolded herself for making such a negative, not to mention unfair, assumption. After all, Javier *hadn't* taken off while she'd slept. He'd merely surprised her by fixing breakfast.

"Can I help?" she asked.

"I've got everything under control, although you could pour us each a cup of coffee."

She strode to the cupboard, pulled out two blue mugs, then filled them with the fresh morning brew. She remembered the decaf she'd made last night and smiled. They'd forgotten all about it in the heat of the moment, so he must have thrown it out this morning and started from scratch.

"Do you take cream or sugar?" she asked as she filled the cups.

"No. I like mine black."

She handed him the first mug, then added a bit of sweetener to hers, as well as a dab of creamer.

As she reached for a spoon, she wondered how

to broach the subject of the future. And to ask one of several questions she had, the most important of which was, "Where do we go from here?"

Instead, she kept things light. "How did you sleep?"

"Not too bad."

That wasn't quite the answer she'd wanted to hear. Not that she expected him to wax on about how wonderful last night had been or how refreshed he'd awakened.

Goodness, she'd only gotten a few hours of sleep herself. But once she'd nodded off, nestled in Javier's arms, she'd slept like a baby.

Again, she tried to shrug off her disappointment, but it wasn't easy.

Was it wrong for her to want to hear him say that making love with her had been every bit as special to him as it had been to her? She didn't think so.

After stirring her coffee and setting the spoon in the sink, she took a sip. Javier certainly knew how to brew a good cup of java. In fact, after last night, she'd learned firsthand some of the other skills he had.

"What do you have going on today?" she asked.

He turned from the stove and faced her, yet he still kept his eye on the eggs. "I've got physical therapy this afternoon. Pete, my therapist, said I could take the weekend off, but I'd rather not. I'm tired of being laid up. It's hell to feel like only half a man."

Her lips quirked into a smile. "You weren't half a man last night."

His eyes sparked and he smiled. Then he returned to watch the pan on the stove, using a spatula to keep the eggs from sticking.

"I thought I'd do some laundry today," she added. "Then I probably ought to run a few errands."

He didn't respond, although she supposed he didn't need to. So she decided to take a more direct approach.

"Would you like to have dinner with me tonight? I thought I could fix chicken."

The light in his eyes dimmed. "I'd like to, but I'm not sure that's a good idea."

What wasn't a good idea? Her stomach clenched. Them having dinner together? Or him returning to her house once he left?

Slow down, she told herself. She was jumping to conclusions. After all, he was fixing breakfast for her. If he'd meant to make a hasty exit, wouldn't he have done so while she'd been sleeping?

Still, her heart, which had been soaring with hope when she first entered the kitchen, sputtered and threatened to stall. "Why isn't it a good idea?"

"Well, because…as good as it was last night—as good as we were together—I think we should take things slowly for now."

He might be right about not rushing into anything, but she couldn't help feeling as though he was giving her the morning-after brush off. And in spite of wanting to give him the benefit of the doubt, she bristled. "I see."

After removing the egg pan from the flame, he turned to face her again, resting his backside against the cupboard. "It's not what you think, baby."

Baby? Under normal circumstances, she might be touched by the term of endearment. But didn't bachelors often refer to their lovers as baby or sweetheart or honey so they didn't have to worry about calling someone by the wrong name?

"Then what should I think?" she asked.

Again he paused, as if choosing his words carefully. And who could blame him? If he wasn't planning to make a commitment, yet wanted to sleep with her again, he'd have to be careful how he handled things now, wouldn't he?

"Last night was great," he said. "*We* were great. But I have a long way to go before I can make any promises or plans for the future."

What was he talking about? Didn't he realize that, at least in some ways, he was as good as he'd ever been? And that even after he was fully healed, she didn't expect perfection?

As badly as she wanted to explain it all away—his attitude, his inability to make a commitment—she realized that she'd been right about him all along. Javier was a playboy bachelor, and there was nothing she could do to change that.

Their romantic night of lovemaking might have meant the world to her. But to him, it had only been the means to an end.

The same thing had happened when she'd dated Jason Novachek, the internist who'd taken her out and charmed her into bed. And while she'd been disappointed that things hadn't worked out the way she'd wanted, that Jason hadn't been the man she'd expected him to be, she hadn't loved him. Not like she...

Oh, God. She took a step back at the realization: she *loved* Javier.

And just like Aunt Connie, she'd fallen hook, line and sinker for a charming but dedicated bachelor whose only real interest in her had been a sexual romp.

Connie had been so devastated by the breakup that she'd never been the same again.

And neither would Leah.

Sure, she was stronger than Aunt Connie. She wouldn't cry and carry on—at least, not in public. She wouldn't go to bed and curl into a fetal position for days on end.

No, Leah would go back to the hospital on Sunday and throw herself into her work. And, with time, she'd get over the pain, over the crushing disappointment.

But when it came to getting involved in another relationship?

She'd trust her instincts next time. And she'd *never*

let some smooth-talking Casanova charm her into bed again.

As badly as she wanted to throw her mug across the kitchen, to hear the ceramic shatter like a heart breaking, to watch the coffee splash and spill down the wall like tears, she held fast to her temper.

And as tempted as she was to scream and demand that Javier get the hell out of her life, she bit her tongue.

After all, she really had no one to blame for any of this but herself. She'd known all along that her handsome patient would recover one day and revert back to the man he'd once been.

Her initial assessment of him had proven to be right. She just hadn't wanted it to be.

"So," she said, "let me see if I understand this. You want to take things slowly until you finish rehab?"

He turned away from the stove to face her again, nodding. "I think it's for the best."

Best for who? Him?

Nevertheless, she continued to lay it on the line. "And you don't want to think about the future until that time?"

He gave a half shrug. "I don't mind thinking about the future. But I don't want to make any plans until I can kiss this cane goodbye."

"And making 'future' plans or commitments includes having dinner with me tonight?"

"You're angry," he said.

No, it was much worse than that. She was ready to throw him and his damn cane out the front door.

He took a step forward. "I care for you, Leah. A lot. And I don't mind dating you."

He didn't *mind?*

She took a step back, maintaining her distance. Then she grabbed hold of the lapels of her robe, holding the edges together, shielding herself from his view. "Maybe you're right, Javier."

He scrunched his face as if he was trying to make sense of her tone, of her words. But a man like him would never understand.

"Once I'm done with rehab," he explained, "we can take up where we left off. It shouldn't be long. A few months maybe. I'll work hard."

Yeah, right. She knew when she was being cut loose. And while she felt the tears welling in her eyes, she refused to cry. Not in front of him.

Take the power position, she'd told Aunt Connie when the attorney told her he wanted to date other women. *Don't call him. Don't grovel. Don't let him think you need him in the least.*

Connie hadn't taken Leah's advice, and look where that had left her.

But Leah wasn't going to let that happen to her. She was going to stand tall. And she was going to end things completely before Javier had the chance to do it himself—whether he'd finished rehab or not.

"You know," she said, "I'm not the least bit hungry.

Instead, I'm going to take a shower and then run those errands I told you about. In the meantime why don't you enjoy your coffee and eggs."

His head cocked to the side, as if he knew she was going to lower the boom. And his instincts were right.

"Just be sure you're gone by the time I'm ready to leave."

Then she turned on her heel and padded out of the kitchen, coffee mug still in her hand.

She might have taken it back to the sink, since her stomach was tied up in so many knots that she wouldn't be able to drink a single drop, but there was no way she'd return and risk undermining the dramatic exit she'd just made.

You'd think that she'd be feeling a little smug, yet disappointment filled her chest. Somewhere, deep inside, she wished that Javier would follow her, that he would stop her and explain that she was wrong, that she'd misunderstood him.

That he loved her, just as she loved him.

But that didn't happen.

As she stepped into the bathroom and closed the door, the tears she'd been holding back began to fill her eyes to the brim until they overflowed and rolled down her cheeks.

Still, she pulled back the shower curtain, turned on the spigot and waited for the noise of the flowing water to drown out any sobs she might make.

Then she dropped to her knees next to the tub and

pressed her hands against her chest—as if that might hold the cracks in her heart from shattering into a million pieces.

Javier had never been asked to leave anyone's house before—especially not that of a woman he'd just made love to. And the fact that the woman in question was Leah made it all the worse.

He'd been tempted to follow her to the bathroom, to knock on the door, to tell her he'd reconsidered. That he wanted to offer himself to her just as he was. And for as long as he lived.

But until he was back on top of his game, he couldn't allow himself to give in. He'd be strapping her with a cripple, and she deserved so much more than that.

When he offered himself to her—body, heart and soul—he would be standing on his own two feet and able to carry her over the threshold. He'd tried to explain that to her.

What if she grew to resent him and his physical limitations? Hell, not a day went by that he didn't resent them himself. Couldn't she see how important it was for them to start out on even footing?

When he'd been in the hospital, Leah had always understood where he was coming from, even when he hadn't come out and said anything.

So why didn't she get it now?

Hell, maybe because he had a hard time wrapping his mind around the reality of it all.

Last night, after the last wave of their climax had ended, after they lay spent in each other's arms, he'd expected to doze off with a sated smile on his face. But he hadn't.

How'd you sleep? she'd asked him earlier.

Not too bad, he'd said. But the truth was, he'd slept like crap. He'd stayed too long at the party last night and had probably overdone it.

He'd been in a lot of pain this morning. So he'd gotten out of bed while she was still asleep, while she couldn't see him reach for his cane, hobble to where he'd left his clothes, then take them to the bathroom.

Once inside, he'd removed his prescription bottle and downed a pain pill before climbing in the shower.

He could have left at that time, he supposed. But when he'd seen her lying in bed, he hadn't been able to go without talking to her this morning. Without explaining why a relationship with him would have to wait. Not until he'd given her his promise to bust his ass in therapy until he was back on top.

But how did that work for you? a small voice asked.

Not good. Not good at all.

Javier glanced down at the eggs he'd fixed, at the fried potatoes he'd placed on a serving platter, ready for someone to eat. And while he'd only munched on appetizers last night, he no longer felt the least bit hungry now.

Instead, he piled everything on one plate and covered it with plastic wrap. Then he put it in her refrigerator.

Next, after he washed the pots and utensils he'd used, he put them back in the cupboard in which he'd found them.

By the time the water had stopped running in the pipes and her shower was apparently over, he had slipped on his sports jacket and was headed for the door.

When he reached for the knob, he had second thoughts about leaving. But only for a moment. Only until he remembered coming through this very door with her last night.

They'd shared a slow dance, wrapped in each other's arms. And when the song had ended, when it had come time to separate, he'd stumbled. And he'd have fallen to the floor if she hadn't offered her support.

If he hadn't been so all-fired enamored with her and so determined to prove that he wasn't a complete cripple, he would have called it a night and limped away.

Instead, he'd proven to her that he could be the man she deserved in bed. And soon, he'd be man enough for her in all the other ways.

He just hoped she'd give him a chance when that day finally came around.

Javier went home long enough to change into his workout clothes, then drove straight to the rehab facility at San Antonio General. He was madder than hell at just about everyone in the world, starting with Mother Nature for sending that blasted tornado through town and having it strike right where he was standing.

And he was angry at Leah for not understanding the one thing that was most important to him.

He needed to be number one in her life, and he couldn't win that position until he'd reached it again in his own.

As he pulled into the parking lot, he found an empty space close to the front door. Then he shut off the ignition, reached across the seat for his gym bag and locked the door.

Once inside, he took a quick scan of the facility and the people inside, noting that Pete hadn't arrived yet. But that didn't matter. Javier knew the routine and would start working out on his own.

He would push himself, too. Even harder than Pete pushed.

After all, he wasn't going to lollygag around and risk having his recovery take longer than necessary. Once he took command of his body and his life again, once he was at a hundred percent, he would set his relationship with Leah back to right.

He would even plan a romantic evening to tell her how he was feeling. He'd never been in love before, but he suspected that's where all of this was heading. His feelings for Leah were too strong not to be the real deal.

"Hey there," Jeremy Fortune called out as he crossed the room to greet Javier. "I'm glad to see you up and around these days. Pete says you're doing great."

Not as great as he'd like to be. But he thanked Jeremy just the same.

"I didn't see you at the open house last night. Kirsten and I arrived late because I was on call and had an emergency. But I heard you and Leah were there."

Javier nodded. "It was a nice party, but we didn't stay very long."

His thoughts drifted to Leah, to the night they'd spent making love. It was only a natural progression to this morning, when everything had come to a head.

"Leah's a great lady," Jeremy said.

That she was. And as wonderful as she was, that lady was pretty damn angry with him right now. He'd never seen her like that, had never suspected she would react like that.

"Are you two dating?" Jeremy asked.

"Not exactly. I have a long way to go before I can think about romance."

"You'd know best," Jeremy said.

That's what Javier kept telling himself. But he'd begun to have his doubts. What if he agreed to have dinner with Leah tonight—assuming she'd accept his apology and reissue the invitation?

And what if they continued to date, even though he wasn't running any marathons yet?

"Well, I'd better go," Jeremy said. "I wanted to check on the progress of one of my other patients, but I need to head back to the office. I have a full afternoon scheduled."

After the men shook hands once again, Javier told his friend and doctor goodbye. Then he began his workout.

He started out slowly, with some stretches and easy exercises. Then he took it a step further, pushing harder, willing his muscles and tendons to strengthen, willing himself to heal.

Working out helped, he decided. It also proved to be a good outlet for his anger and frustration.

As he pushed through the pain, as he fought to become whole once again, his breath came out in ragged huffs. Perspiration beaded upon his brow.

His head grew light.

Still, he didn't let up.

He didn't quit.

As he moved from one of the chair exercises to another, his knees shook, wobbled. His vision blurred, and without warning he found himself falling.

His ears were ringing, but he heard someone yell, "Call for Dr. Fortune. *Stat!*"

As Javier collapsed, his head struck something hard, and everything went black.

Chapter Twelve

After Leah returned home from running her errands, she parked her car in the garage. Then she entered the house through the laundry room.

She might have had the last word with Javier this morning and taken the power position, but she'd never once felt like the winner. Not when she'd lost what few hopes and dreams she'd dared to harbor.

From the time she'd holed up in the bathroom this morning, with the water running to hide her cries, she'd tried to make sense of it all.

How could he make love to her like that—with a slow hand that seemed to know all the right places to touch, to stroke, to caress? It had seemed as though her needs and desires had been more important to him that night than his own. Yet he'd given her every reason to believe that she'd been an amazing lover, too.

She supposed he'd had a lot of practice with that sort of thing. But that didn't make losing him any easier.

Even when she'd dressed and returned to the kitchen, she'd held the briefest of hopes that he would be waiting for her, that he'd be eager to explain, to tell her the words she'd wanted to hear.

But she'd found him gone, the dishes washed and put away as if he'd never been there at all.

Yet he'd been there all right. She had an ache in her heart and a fist-size knot in her stomach to prove it.

It was nearing lunchtime now, but she still wasn't any hungrier than she'd been this morning when she'd told him to leave.

After making two trips to the car to bring in all of the shopping bags, she began to put everything where it belonged—frozen food in the freezer, perishables in the fridge and canned goods in the pantry.

She'd just folded the recyclable shopping bags and put them away when the telephone rang.

She closed the cupboard door, then answered on the second ring. "Hello?"

"Leah? I hope I'm not bothering you, but this is Pete Hopkins from the rehab unit."

She stiffened. Why would Javier's PT call her at home?

"What can I do for you?" she asked.

"I'm afraid there's been a little accident."

Her heart, which she'd thought had already been broken beyond measure, dropped to the floor. "What are you talking about? What happened?"

"Javier Mendoza collapsed while working out today. We rushed him to the E.R., and they've admitted him for observation."

"Oh, my God. How did that happen?"

"I wish I could tell you, but I wasn't there at the time. From what I understand, he didn't get much sleep last night. He also went without breakfast this morning, so his blood sugar was low. Then he pushed himself too hard in therapy. When he fell, he hit his head on the floor and blacked out."

His head? Oh, no. She grabbed her purse and keys before hearing anything else.

"Is he going to be all right?" she asked.

"I hope so. You'll have to talk to Dr. Fortune, who was the first to arrive in rehab. He called in the resident neurologist to make sure."

"Thanks, Pete. I'll be right there."

"Dr. Fortune thought you'd say that."

She didn't give a whole lot of thought about what Dr. Fortune might have said or why. She just knew that she had to get to the hospital.

And she had to see Javier for herself.

Javier lay on a gurney in the E.R., awaiting word that he'd been admitted to San Antonio General.

He was lucky, he supposed. His collapse and fall hadn't caused any permanent damage. But because of the head injury and the surgery he'd had in January, the neurologist ordered a CT scan and made the decision to keep him overnight for observation.

After Javier had passed out on the rehab floor, Jeremy had rushed to his aid, then had him placed on a gurney and taken to the E.R. And while he had a good-size knot on his head, Javier had come to fairly quickly, although things had been abuzz for a while. But he'd been assured that he hadn't suffered anything more than a mild concussion.

"You shouldn't be pushing yourself so hard," Jeremy had told him once the crisis was over.

"I'm sick and tired of being laid up. I want to get better."

"You *are* better, Javier. And each day you make a little more progress toward a full recovery. But you can't expect any more miracles than the one you've already had."

Javier figured that Jeremy was talking about the fact that he'd nearly died those first days after the tornado. Yet he'd still lived to tell about it. And he was probably right. The doctors and specialists who'd met with his family had all given them the same advice: hope for the best, but be prepared for the worst.

"Don't forget that there were some serious concerns about brain damage after the head injury you suffered. And at that point, your internal injuries and fractures had only been minor inconveniences in the scheme of things." Jeremy crossed his arms. "Who's been pushing you so hard?"

"No one. Just me."

Jeremy clucked his tongue and shook his head. "Then I'll give you the same advice I'd give anyone else who'd encouraged you to work out that hard. And on an empty stomach at that. *Knock it off.* You've got several more months of therapy ahead of you, and as long as you give it your all—letting Pete be the one to push you—you'll be fine. But if you refuse to listen to medical advice and continue with that macho attitude of yours, you might end up suffering a major setback. And then where will that leave you?"

In a place much worse than the one he was in right now, he supposed.

"Before you know it, probably by the end of summer, you'll be back on the golf course and flying across the country, wheeling and dealing again."

"You think so?" Javier asked, wishing it was sooner but glad to have some kind of date to set his sights on.

"Unless you try to rush the natural course of things. And if that happens, then it's anyone's guess."

"I'll take it easy," Javier said. "But tell me, Doc. What are the odds of me making a complete and full recovery by…say, September?"

"I'd say a hundred to one."

"Six months, huh?"

"Can you deal with that?"

When Javier nodded his agreement, Jeremy patted him on the shoulder, then glanced out the door. "I'm going to call for an orderly."

Jeremy had no more than stepped away from the gurney when someone else approached. But not just any someone.

It was Leah.

And she looked like hell. Her hair was windblown, her face was pale.

"What's the matter?" he asked.

"You're asking *me?*" Her pretty hazel eyes grew wide. "What in the world happened to you?"

"I told you I didn't like being laid up, so I was trying to hurry things along."

"That was a crazy thing to do."

"Yeah, that's what my orthopedic surgeon just told me—at least in so many words." Javier gave a little shrug, then studied the nurse who wasn't on duty today, yet obviously came running to the E.R. on a moment's notice. And the fact that she had almost made his collapse from exhaustion worthwhile.

"How did you know where I was?" he asked.

"Pete called me. Apparently, Jeremy thought I should know."

"Thanks for coming. I'm glad you did."

"You are? Why is that?"

Javier wasn't sure what he should say at this point. *I'm sorry* came to mind. And so did *We need to talk.*

Instead, he said, "Because you've been the best friend I've ever had. And the fact that you've been so annoyed with me, yet you still cared enough to come see about me proves that I'm your friend, too."

She paused for a beat, then crossed her arms. "Pete said you missed breakfast. And then you overdid it during your therapy workout. What in the world were you trying to do? Kill yourself?"

He liked that spark of life that lit her eyes—even when it had been fueled by anger, like it had been this morning.

"I wasn't lying when I told you that I didn't want to make a commitment to you until I was completely healed."

"And that's why you pushed yourself so hard?" She appeared skeptical.

"I was also trying to get well enough to tell you something I probably should have admitted this morning."

"What's that?"

Damn. It had come to mind so easily before. Why was he having such a difficult time confessing it now?

He took in a deep, fortifying breath, then said, "When I told you that I wanted to take things slowly, it wasn't because I was questioning what I felt for you or because I wanted to see other women. You're the only one I want to be with—now or in the future."

Her lips parted and her head cocked slightly to the side.

He supposed she didn't understand what he was getting at. Did he have to spell it out and tell her he loved her when he hadn't quite gotten used to the idea himself?

"I'll make a commitment to you just as soon as I can carry you to bed. I don't want to have to rely on you to get me there."

"You didn't need any help once you were lying down," she said. "And I hope you're not saying that you don't want to make love again until you can run a footrace."

"No, I'm not saying that. I want to see you, to be with you, to sleep with you. It's just that..." Hell, right this minute, it didn't seem to matter anymore.

"Why would your physical condition even come into play?" she asked. "I consider you whole—with or without that cane."

"Thanks, I appreciate that. But before we start talking about rings and that sort of thing, I not only want to be walking on my own, I want to be back at work, buying and selling property, turning a profit, investing. And I'm just not there yet."

"So why didn't you just come out and say that this morning?"

"I couldn't admit it, I guess. Maybe because you deserve so much more than the man I am right now. But I swear to you, honey. I'll be that man again before you know it. Jeremy said it would take another six months. Can you wait for me?"

"Are you *kidding?*" She crossed her arms and scrunched her brow.

Why would he kid about something like that? His feelings for her and the fear of losing her for good were all he'd been thinking about since leaving her house this morning.

"You mean to tell me that you don't want to have anything to do with me for six months?" she asked, her eyes sparking again, the furrow in her brow deepening.

"I didn't say that." In fact, after making love with her, he wasn't so sure he wanted to wait more than a day or two for another repeat of their romantic evening.

"But you turned down my dinner invitation tonight," she reminded him. "Why is that?"

"I don't know. Mostly because I needed some time to sort through all that I'm feeling for you. So I didn't want to rush into things. It seemed like the right idea at the time."

"How does it sound now?"

"Not so good, Leah. I want to have dinner with you every night for the rest of my life. I think I'm falling in love with you."

The furrow that had marred her brow disappeared, and she unfolded her arms. As her eyes sought his, she reached for his forehead, where he now sported a nasty bump thanks to the fall, and carefully probed around the tender spot with gentle fingers.

Did she think that having his brain jarred again had caused him to imagine feelings he didn't have? If so, he needed to set her straight. "Leah, I've been falling for you for a long time—probably since the first day you walked into my room and introduced yourself. But I've never said those words to anyone other than my family members. So no, it didn't just roll off my tongue without a whole lot of forethought and consideration."

A smile stretched across her face, lighting her eyes.

Did that mean she was going to cut him some slack? He sure hoped so.

"I've never felt this way before," he added, "so all of this is new to me. I'm bound to say the wrong thing on occasion. But I'll get it right. I promise."

"You're not the only one who's on uncharted ground. I'm afraid to lay my heart on the line and have it thrown back at me."

"Is that what you thought I was doing this morning? Throwing your feelings right back at you?"

"Weren't you?"

He really hadn't meant to do that. "I'm sorry, Leah. When I get out of here, we can go back to your house and do things right."

"I'd like that," she said. "To be honest, I've probably been a little too sensitive. Ever since a couple of your old girlfriends came to visit you in the hospital, I realized that I could never compete with them. And I was afraid that when you fully recovered and regained your strength, you'd revert back to the man you were and the life you had before."

"First of all, for the record, those women could never compete with you in any respect, honey. You'd blow them out of the water. And secondly, other than having stiff and aching legs, I'm still that same guy."

Leah seemed to think on that for a moment, as though she needed to let his words and the reality sink in before she believed it.

But then again, Javier needed to let those words sink in, too.

Other than having stiff and aching legs, I'm still that same guy.

As the truth struck home, something clicked inside. Something he'd struggled with for far too long. He wasn't perfect—and it didn't matter that he wasn't. He didn't have to prove anything to anyone, especially not to Leah.

He might have suffered some physical setbacks, but deep down inside his heart, he was still the same man he'd always been.

"So what do you think?" he asked. "Can you give the old me with bum legs and a cane another chance?"

"I'd been afraid that you were the worst guy in the world for me to fall in love with."

"And what do you think now?"

"That you're probably the best." Then she bent down and placed a loving kiss on his lips.

After she straightened, she added, "As much as I'd

like to stay and talk to you more about this, I'm going to take off and let you get some rest. That's why Dr. Fortune wanted you to stay the night."

"All right. But I need to clarify one more thing."

"What's that?"

"You didn't actually say that you were falling for me, too."

"I tried my best not to, but I'm afraid I fell head over heels in love with you the day they wheeled you into your room on the third floor."

He slid a boyish grin her way. "Even before I could get out of bed on my own?"

"Even when you were snippy and moody with your family." She reached for his hand and gave it a squeeze. "I don't want a perfect man, Javier. I just want you."

He laughed. "Why do I get the feeling that you meant that as a compliment?"

"Because I did."

Before he could respond, the orderly showed up to take Javier to his room.

"I'm getting out of here tomorrow," Javier told Leah. "And since you're not working, will you pick me up?"

"I'd be happy to."

"Great. As soon as they get the paperwork in order, I'll give you a call and let you know when to come."

"All right. But why don't I just come early? I can hang out with you until you're released."

"No, I'd rather you waited for me to call. But I wouldn't mind having you fix that dinner you were going to make for me tonight."

"All right. You've got it. Should I plan on having you stay over for breakfast, too?"

"I'd be disappointed if you didn't."

When he finally reached his room, she kissed him again—this time as a goodbye. "I'd stay, but you need to get some rest."

She was right about that. He also wanted to have a minute to himself. He had a couple of phone calls to make in preparation for what he planned to do when she came for him tomorrow.

When Leah arrived at San Antonio General to take Javier home, she spotted Luis Mendoza in the lobby and stopped to greet the man, who was grinning from ear to ear.

"How's he doing?" she asked.

"He's got a bump on his noggin, but other than that, I don't think I've ever seen him better." Then Luis reached out and took both of Leah's hands in his, giving them a warm clasp before letting them go. "He said you're going to take him home. And I think that's really nice."

Okay. Something seemed a little off. But maybe it's because she hadn't ever seen Javier's father so happy. Had he and Javier received good news?

She made her way to the elevator, then took it up to the third floor.

But when she entered 310, the room he'd been assigned last night, she found his bed empty. So she went to the nurses' station, where Brenna sat.

"Where's Javier?" she asked.

Brenna burst into a grin nearly as bright as the one Luis had worn. "Dr. Fortune took him outside in a wheelchair. And they said to tell you, if you came looking for him, that you'd find him in the rose garden."

After thanking Brenna, Leah made her way to the garden.

She only walked a short way before spotting Javier sitting on one of the benches, his cane resting beside him. In his hands, he held his guitar.

Is that why Luis had been smiling? Because Javier had asked for his guitar?

That seemed like an odd request, especially since he was supposed to be going home today, but she decided not to dwell on it. Instead, she approached the bench on which Javier sat.

She hadn't seen it at first, but a glass vase filled with red roses sat at his feet.

"What's going on?" she asked.

He strummed a couple of chords, then asked her to take a seat. As she did so, he began to play a familiar tune—Anne Murray's "Could I Have This Dance."

She'd always loved that song and had heard it used

at several weddings. As Javier sang the words as though they'd been written especially for her, asking her to dance with him for the rest of his life, her heart swelled to the point that she thought she might float away.

And she found herself falling in love with him all over again.

When he'd sung his heart out, when the beautiful words had rung true, her eyes filled with tears.

"I'd wanted to wait to ask you to be my wife until I was back to fighting weight. And Jeremy assures me that I'll be as good as new by fall. So I was wondering how you'd feel about a September wedding?"

She couldn't believe he was doing this for her, sharing his talent, touching her heart.

"I think that would be perfect. Do you have a day in mind?"

"No, I'll let you settle on one. And while you're at it, why don't you see if you can take a couple weeks off for a honeymoon."

"I'm sure that I can. I've got a lot of time on the books." Up until this point, she'd been so focused on work that she had a lot of vacations she'd failed to take.

"Then marry me, Leah. Be my friend, my lover, my wife."

The tears welled in her eyes, and as she nodded her answer, one droplet slid down her cheek, followed by another. "Yes," she finally managed to say. "I'll marry you, Javier."

He placed the guitar to the side, then wrapped her in his arms and kissed her with all the love in his heart.

When the kiss ended, when they came up for air in the garden where Leah had first dreamed of having a home and family of her own, she realized that Javier had just made her dreams come true—and in such a wonderful, romantic way.

"I love you," she said. "More than you'll ever know."

"I've got a pretty good idea, honey. Because I love you more than I ever thought possible." He glanced at his watch. "Come on, we'd better get home before the phone starts ringing."

"Are you expecting a call?"

"A whole slew of them. You see, my dad brought my guitar and the bouquet of roses to me this morning."

"So he knows about this, about us?"

"Yes, and he's probably spread the news to everyone in the family by now."

"I hope they'll be happy."

"They'll be thrilled," he said. "And they'll probably start gearing up for our big day in September. So I hope you like big weddings."

"I'll like ours."

Then right there, in the center of the hospital rose

garden, with new blooms bursting with new life, Javier kissed Leah again. When their kiss ended, Leah said, "Come on. Let's go home."

"There's nothing I'd like better." As he reached for his cane, he wobbled a bit. She stood by to grab him if he needed her to, but she didn't make an issue of it.

"You know," Javier said, as they started down the walkway. "Jeremy mentioned that my survival after that tornado had been nothing short of a miracle."

"That's true," she said.

"And he implied that miracles are often a once-in-a-lifetime occurrence. But next time I see him, I'm going to tell him he's wrong."

"What makes you say that?"

"Because I've been more fortunate than most people ever are. I've experienced two of them within the past three months. And falling in love with you and having you love me back is the biggest miracle of all."

He was right about that.

Leah slipped her free hand into Javier's and walked toward the parking lot where she'd left her car.

She'd been blessed beyond measure, too.

What they'd found in each other's arms was nothing short of miraculous. And she planned to love and cherish him for the rest of her life.

* * * * *

HEART & HOME

Heartwarming romances where love can
happen right when you least expect it.

Harlequin®
SPECIAL EDITION®

You can find more information on upcoming Harlequin® titles,
free excerpts and more at www.HarlequinInsideRomance.com.

REQUEST YOUR FREE BOOKS!
2 FREE NOVELS PLUS 2 FREE GIFTS!

♦ Harlequin®

SPECIAL EDITION
Life, Love & Family

YES! Please send me 2 FREE Harlequin® Special Edition novels and my 2 FREE gifts (gifts are worth about $10). After receiving them, if I don't wish to receive any more books, I can return the shipping statement marked "cancel." If I don't cancel, I will receive 6 brand-new novels every month and be billed just $4.49 per book in the U.S. or $5.24 per book in Canada. That's a saving of at least 14% off the cover price! It's quite a bargain! Shipping and handling is just 50¢ per book in the U.S. and 75¢ per book in Canada.* I understand that accepting the 2 free books and gifts places me under no obligation to buy anything. I can always return a shipment and cancel at any time. Even if I never buy another book, the two free books and gifts are mine to keep forever.

235/335 HDN FEGF

Name _____ (PLEASE PRINT)

Address _____ Apt. #

City _____ State/Prov. _____ Zip/Postal Code

Signature (if under 18, a parent or guardian must sign)

Mail to the **Reader Service:**
IN U.S.A.: P.O. Box 1867, Buffalo, NY 14240-1867
IN CANADA: P.O. Box 609, Fort Erie, Ontario L2A 5X3

Not valid for current subscribers to Harlequin Special Edition books.

Want to try two free books from another line?
Call 1-800-873-8635 or visit www.ReaderService.com.

* Terms and prices subject to change without notice. Prices do not include applicable taxes. Sales tax applicable in N.Y. Canadian residents will be charged applicable taxes. Offer not valid in Quebec. This offer is limited to one order per household. All orders subject to credit approval. Credit or debit balances in a customer's account(s) may be offset by any other outstanding balance owed by or to the customer. Please allow 4 to 6 weeks for delivery. Offer available while quantities last.

Your Privacy—The Reader Service is committed to protecting your privacy. Our Privacy Policy is available online at www.ReaderService.com or upon request from the Reader Service.

We make a portion of our mailing list available to reputable third parties that offer products we believe may interest you. If you prefer that we not exchange your name with third parties, or if you wish to clarify or modify your communication preferences, please visit us at www.ReaderService.com/consumerschoice or write to us at Reader Service Preference Service, P.O. Box 9062, Buffalo, NY 14269. Include your complete name and address.

HSE11B

*It's never too late for love
in Hope's Crossing...*

**A charming tale of romance and community
by *USA TODAY* bestselling author**

RaeAnne Thayne

"Romance, vivid characters and a wonderful story; really,
who could ask for more?"
—Debbie Macomber, #1 *New York Times* bestselling author,
on *Blackberry Summer*

Woodrose Mountain

Coming in April 2012!

www.Harlequin.com

PHRT660CS

Taft Bowman knew he'd ruined any chance he'd had for happiness with Laura Pendleton when he drove her away years ago...and into the arms of another man, thousands of miles away. Now she was back, a widow with two small children...and despite himself, he was starting to believe in second chances.

Harlequin Special® Edition® presents a new installment in USA TODAY *bestselling author RaeAnne Thayne's miniseries,* THE COWBOYS OF COLD CREEK.

Enjoy a sneak peek of
A COLD CREEK REUNION

Available April 2012 from Harlequin® Special Edition®

A younger woman stood there, and from this distance he had only a strange impression, as though she was somehow standing on an island of calm amid the chaos of the scene, the flashing lights of the emergency vehicles, shouts between his crew members, the excited buzz of the crowd.

And then the woman turned and he just about tripped over a snaking fire hose somebody shouldn't have left there.

Laura.

He froze, and for the first time in fifteen years as a firefighter, he forgot about the incident, his mission, just what the hell he was doing here.

Laura.

Ten years. He hadn't seen her in all that time, since the week before their wedding when she had given him back his ring and left town. Not just town. She had left the whole damn country, as if she couldn't run far enough to get away from him.

Some part of him desperately wanted to think he had made some kind of mistake. It couldn't be her. That was just some other slender woman with a long sweep of honey-blond hair and big, blue, unforgettable eyes. But no. It was definitely Laura. Sweet and lovely.

Not his.

He was going to have to go over there and talk to her. He didn't want to. He wanted to stand there and pretend he hadn't seen her. But he was the fire chief. He couldn't hide out just because he had a painful history with the daughter of the property owner.

Sometimes he hated his job.

Will Taft and Laura be able to make the years recede...or is the gulf between them too broad to ever cross?

Find out in
A COLD CREEK REUNION
Available April 2012 from Harlequin® Special Edition®
wherever books are sold.

Celebrate the 30th anniversary
of Harlequin® Special Edition® with a bonus story
included in each Special Edition® book in April!

Copyright © 2012 by RaeAnne Thayne

Harlequin® *Romance*

*Get swept away with a brand-new miniseries
by* **USA TODAY** *bestselling author*

MARGARET WAY

The Langdon Dynasty

Amelia Norton knows that in order to embrace her future,
she must first face her past. As she unravels her family's secrets,
she is forced to turn to gorgeous cattleman Dev Langdon for
support—the man she vowed never to fall for again.

Against the haze of the sweltering Australian heat Mel's
guarded exterior begins to crumble...and Dev will do
whatever it takes to convince his childhood sweetheart
to be his bride.

THE CATTLE KING'S BRIDE
Available April 2012

And look for
ARGENTINIAN IN THE OUTBACK
Coming in May 2012

www.Harlequin.com

HR17799